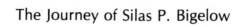

The Journey of Silas P. Bigelow

THE JOURNEY OF SILAS P. BIGELOW

by Kenan Heise

ILLUSTRATED BY
SCOTT HOLINGUE

COLLAGE, INC.

Copyright © 1981 Kenan Heise

All rights reserved.

Published by Collage, Inc.
1200 S. Willis Avenue
Wheeling, Illinois 60090

Library of Congress Catalog Card No. 80-70749

ISBN No. 0-938728-00-8

Printed in the United States of America

First Edition

Editorial Production by Bookcrafters

Jacket Design by John Von Dorn

Printed and bound by WHITEHALL COMPANY

To those who suffer
and still find a way
to hope.

Contents

Acknowledgments

This book already has a lot of friends. Some of them are: Gene De Roin, its editor and nurturer; Carol, who gave me time and encouragement; Al Schenk, Joe Pete, and Gayle Simmons, who each shared a part of their Indian heritage; Virgil Vogel, a man of ideals and of history; Sheri Steinberg, Lee Sandlin, Gayle Altur, and Alison James, who supported and criticized; John and Susan McCutcheon, who offered the hospitality of their house on the tall-grass prairie; and finally, Scott Holingue, who drew so well.

The Journey of Silas P. Bigelow

Preface

This book attempts to answer the question: "What kind of native American civilization would have evolved in the old Northwest Territory if it had been allowed to develop unhindered?" In Kenan Heise's story, the Treaty of Paris, which ended the Revolutionary War in 1783, confined the United States to the seaboard states and created an Indian Nation in the land bounded by the Great Lakes, the Ohio, and Mississippi Rivers. In actual history, the Indians were ignored in the treaty, and this region became American soil due to George Rogers Clark's conquest. It was eventually carved into five states: Ohio, Indiana, Michigan, Illinois, Wisconsin, and part of a sixth, Minnesota. But it almost didn't happen that way.

Our history books gloss over the reality that our second war with Great Britain in 1812 was very nearly a defeat for the United States, and when peace negotiations began at Ghent, then part of the Netherlands, on August 8, 1814, they dragged on nearly three and a half months, until Christmas eve, during which time American reverses included the burning of Washington while Jackson's victory at New Orleans came too late to affect the treaty.

The British negotiators pressed the Americans, led by John Quincy Adams, to agree that the whole Northwest Territory should constitute a demilitarized Indian buffer state so that Canada might be secure from American attacks. Adams insisted that there was no way to achieve that except by a war of utter extermination, whereupon the British eventually yielded. Still, the Americans had to accept the humiliating Article IX, which required the United States to make a separate peace with each Indian nation allied to Britain and "to restore to such tribes or nations, respectively, all the possessions, rights, and privileges" which they had before the war. A similar clause applied also to Britain, but only for the appearance of equality in the terms.

The consequence of Article IX was that the dispossession of these tribes from their remaining lands had to be put off to a later series of treaties with the Illinois, Kickapoo, Miami, Shawnee, Sauk and Fox, Wyandot, and Winnebago tribes, extending into the 1840's. The eventful result was that no tribal land remained in Ohio, Indiana, or Illinois, and the aboriginal inhabitants were removed to Nebraska, Kansas, and Oklahoma. In the still undesired wilderness of northern Michigan, Wisconsin, and Minnesota, the original owners, mostly Ojibwa, Ottawa, Menominee, and Potawatomi Indians, were reduced to possession of small and scattered reservations where they still remain.

If the British had won their argument at Ghent, how would the American Indian culture in the buffer region have evolved? How much of the old values could have been retained in a large, social island surrounded by a burgeoning white nation committed to technological growth, competition, acquisitiveness, and the conquest of man and nature, in contrast to the harmony with nature, cooperative, and non-material bent of the Indian Nation? The clash of cultures in other parts of the world suggests an answer. Political boundaries seldom keep out trade, and trade is the battering ram that has turned every so-called underdeveloped region into an economic appendage of the developed world, and thence into political colonies. Japan was almost alone in preserving its independence against the onslaught of trade, but she did so only by quickly adopting the technology of the expansionists.

This process was well advanced among the Indians by 1812. Most of them were not simply hunters; long before the whites came, they also had been farmers. About 45 percent of all the farm produce in America today consists of crops once grown by Indians, including corn, beans, pumpkins, squash, and tobacco. When Europeans came, they wanted furs, and the Indians increased their hunting (and fighting) to meet this demand, spurred by their desire for firearms, axes, knives, kettles, cloth, and other manufactures bartered for skins. Soon they were depleting an important part of their own subsistence and becoming more dependent on the alien economy. Some understood what was happening, though none could reverse it. As Indian agent, Thomas Forsyth, wrote of the Sauks and Foxes in 1827:

> The Indians admire our manufactories, but more particularly guns and gunpowder, but many old Indians say they were more happy before they knew the use of fire arms, because, they then could kill as much game as they wanted, not being compelled to destroy game to purchase our merchandise as they are now obliged to do.

So, if we may judge by what we know about the demolishing impact of industrialism on non-industrial peoples, it is improbable that the Indians would have been able to resist all of it. And if living value systems (as distinguished from forgotten ones frozen in sacred books) reflect the material environment, it is probable that Indian values and customs would have undergone devastating change even in a sovereign Indian state. It seems unlikely then, that Silas P. Bigelow, the protagonist in this book, would have found that the Indian Nation had managed to keep itself tightly closed to intrusion from Western civilization.

But this book is not a text on anthropology, economics, history, politics, or sociology, though it reflects study of all of these. In imagining what might have happened in an autonomous Amerindian culture, it is not necessary to assume that it would have happened under certain conditions or even that it could have happened under any conditions. This book does something more than speculate about the "ifs" of history. What it does, by indirection, is to examine the flaws, or even the validity, of our own society. We need to stand back at times and look at our own culture through the eyes of another, even a fictional character. This book does that, and thus it is in the great tradition of Thomas More's *Utopia* (1516), Jonathan Swift's *Gulliver's Travels* (1726), and Edward Bellamy's *Looking Backward* (1888), each of which tried to show what the imperfect societies of the authors might be, by transporting the reader to another society founded on different principles. In this book Silas P. Bigelow, a journalist, comes to Chicagou, the metropolis of the Indian Nation, to write a story on what the Indian Nation would have been like if it had been part of the United States for the last 200 years. Instead, he becomes a learner and in the end sees America as a land of "abundance and waste," where "emotions came from hoping for a few more dollars or a few more meaningless objects."

Questions are raised here that deserve better examination than they usually receive. What is progress, and how is it measured? "The Chicagou Indians do not repudiate it," we are told, "but neither do they evaluate it with the same weights and measures Western civilization does." The Indians had "forged a strong, successful culture that is a mixture of science and respect for their past." It was, says Silas Bigelow, "nature come to fruition; man, free and unharassed by war, achieving something new and creative in a variety of human endeavors in art, architecture, politics, and psychology." It was a society where time was not precisely measured, and so the visitor put his watch aside. There were no locks on doors, for none were needed. Buildings were made of local materials and merged with their surroundings. Conservation of soil, clean streams and air, were all taken for granted. Ecology and the unity of man and nature is a constant theme. Currency played a minor role in the economy; there were no banks. Profit was not a goal in trade; caring for and feeding people were. In the grain "pit," or market, a leading man negotiated; in return for several shiploads of wheat, the Indians "received" "a medical library, farm implements, and the stipulation that the French trading company would send one-third of the shipment free to an African tribe."

But this is no blueprint for a particular system; it offers no finely detailed structure. Only the outlines are there, for a people-centered society, with the focus on values rather than "systems." Unlike preceding books of its genre, this one deals with the quality of personal relations between people—between men and women and between generations. Here the theme is freedom and equality, not possession or domination. The word "sharing" is frequently used to describe the essence of human relations.

Our narrator, Silas Bigelow, is able to bridge the gulf between cultures through his attraction to Ojuiba, a young Potawatomi woman who is stimulating to his mind and spirit, as well as his physical being. She is capable of such insightful remarks as, "your people know as much and understand so little." On the tall-grass prairie they come together, and there the story reaches a fitting, if tragic, climax.

What Kenan Heise has created here is not a sermon or a tract and certainly not a pedantic lecture, but a story of personal adventure into which is woven challenging questions about the quality of our public and private lives. But in all of this, *the dramatis personae* are not submerged in verbiage; their characters as human beings are always visible.

As an historian and social scientist it is not my role to furnish a literary evaluation of this book. I can say that it reflects serious study of American Indian history and customs, though it does not pretend to portray them with the systematic exactitude of an anthropologist in the field or an historian in the archives. What it offers an ordinary reader is an entertaining excursion into an imaginary but not unimaginable world where dreams can become real.

That, it seems to me, is enough for any book to do.

Virgil J. Vogel
Fall, 1980

The passenger pigeon...warm and
alive as if from God's
own private collection

Chapter 1

A Sanctuary on Lake Michiganin

I am in jail: a colorless cubicle that is trying to crowd me. "Protective custody" the United States Army is calling it. I am its hostage. I know too much.

Anger! Its rumblings are deep. They shoot pain into my heart and into my throat as I relive what has happened.

I also feel free. The bars on the window are not real. The walls are not winning their persistent battle against me. I am enveloped, rather, by the boundlessness of the tall-grass prairies of the Indian Nation.

I have been there. Birds, passenger pigeons, swirl over my head. These birds swoop and dart. They overwhelm my consciousness, sweeping away other memories of my tumultous journey to Chicagou and the Indian Nation.

I have been there. I became part of Chicagou. I was at the vortex of its cataclysm. The storm has gone. I feel passive, subdued.

The birds insist on telling their story before I begin mine. I will let them.

The dominant Chicagou bird is the exquisite passenger pigeon, also called the wild pigeon. Here in the United States, east of the Allegheny Mountains, it is extinct. Not a solitary one can be found, not in zoo, aviary, or game preserve. Yet the lands to the west, protected for and by the Indians, are home to flocks of tens of thousands of these pigeons, birds that survive only in a country where the natural bounty has been preserved.

Two hundred years are gone since 1783. The Treaty of Paris ended the Revolutionary War and divided the United States and the Indian Nation. The differences are accentuated by the fate in each land

1

of the passenger pigeon. Man can exist without freedom. This bird, seemingly, cannot.

In Chicagou I watched wild birds perform and dance in multitudes. They made a thunderous racket as they beat the air and yelled to proclaim their existence. Alighting by the thousands, they dominated the trees and the earth as they had the skies.

In their numbers they could blot out the sky. Yet, a single bird could catch your eye, an elegant and fascinating creature. I held a wild pigeon, an injured one, in my hand and felt it to be a piece of very fine china, though warm and alive as if from God's private collection. It cooed, almost purred with vitality, commanding attention and respect. I'm neither bird lover nor watcher, just a person hypnotized by this minute item on the shelf of life's realities.

They fly low, skim and undulate over the landscape. No bird—except the eagle in its dive—is as fast. I saw passenger pigeons dart unerringly, quicker than a thought, through the woods. Nature has stored up in this bird special resources of exceptional speed, beauty, grace, and proliferation to help it survive the onslaughts of winter, hunter, and eclectic misfortune.

Until recent events, no passenger pigeon in the Indian Nation had ever heard the echoed thunder of a rifle or the clap of a pistol. No sportsman felt the easy squeeze of a trigger that could bag dozens of birds in one shotgun blast. Simply, the Indian Nation was successful in its 200-year struggle to become a haven for both Indian and wildlife.

In the 20 states that comprise the United States, a challenge solidified—oh, so angrily—into the "American Fairness Doctrine." The central thrust argued that it was right and it was fair for the country to expand westward at the expense of the Indian Nation, which produced a surplus of meat, grain, copper, and iron. The other nations of the world—since these commodities have been generously shared by the Indians—have been united in opposition to westward expansion by the United States.

Early this year I was given the assignment as a journalist to visit the Indian Nation. Specifically, I was to hypothesize in a series of articles about what the Indian Nation would be like if it had been part of the United States for the past 200 years. I do not claim to have been ideally suited for this role. Simply, my editor offered me the job, and I accepted enthusiastically. I was to be the first American reporter to journey to the Indian Nation in decades.

Speculators wrote and offered a thousand schemes for me to suggest to the Indian councils, ways to make more money and advance the cause of mankind simultaneously. "All" these writers asked was that they be allowed to offer their expertise to the Indians. One bizarre scheme was to turn a stretch of Lake Michiganin shore into a cemetery so that Americans who wanted to migrate to the Indian Nation could at least do so after death. This presumably would save room in U. S. cities, and the Indians certainly would not have to fear being overrun by the dead. The footnote on the letter was an urgent: "I await your promise that you will propose this idea to them."

Business people were not the only ones to approach me. Unofficial representatives of the U. S. government also sought to "brief" me. The issue constantly was referred to as "sensitive." The honest description was "explosive." Pressure for expansion westward had not subsided for 200 years. Politicians came up with tactics and new arguments constantly. Each new generation had to deal with it, and about once every 20 years the situation became ugly.

Signs indicated it was headed in that direction again on the two hundredth anniversary of the 1783 Treaty. The United States was crouched—the word cannot be too strong—for attack as I blithely set off for Chicagou.

Only later would I learn that an out-of-uniform intelligence officer, Major Dick Thoreau, whom I met briefly, proposed sending into the Indian Nation an American citizen "cloaked in innocence and ignorance."

A century before, hunters used a similar tactic to capture and kill thousands of passenger pigeons, blinding one by lacing its eyelids shut, then attaching it to a long pole, or "stool," to lure other birds into a large net.

I was to be my country's "stool pigeon," part of a very sophisticated and deadly trap.

They attempted to conceal nothing.

Chapter 2

Chicagou

Dawn broke behind my canoe on a mild Lake Michiganin. Its reflection shimmered and glistened on the water and on the village of Chicagou. This before me seemed more a forest than a settlement of 500,000. As my paddle momentarily rested, my senses absorbed this home of the descendants of the Miami, Potawatomi, Chippewa, and Ottawa. The hypnotic symmetry might have landscaped a dream, or even some secret fantasy of nature. No building reached above the tallest tree in the silhouetted scene that offered only muted shades between the light and the dark, the natural and the man-made. In the shadows, I projected hazily the depth of its past and the elusiveness of its future.

The Indians say that spirits, souls of people living and dead, patrol their borders. I might then and there have been in the presence of the Potawatomi, Black Partridge; the Shawnee, Tecumseh; or the Sauk, Black Hawk. Perhaps I was being guided into this new world by the ethereal presence of the very much alive and tender woman I was to encounter, Ojuiba.

My canoe had weaned away from the sloop on which I had arrived. I again took up paddle toward the early awakening Chicagou. My mind focused on my writing assignment for the *Philadelphia Gazette*: What would Chicagou be like had 200 years ago the 1783 Treaty of Paris put these northwest lands under control of the colonial United States? Under Britain's wing as an Indian protectorate, they had blossomed more than 100 years ago into the independent Indian Nation. Success and prosperity, combined with the leadership of men such as Tecumseh, welded together a strong nation that discarded the tomahawk and adopted as its symbol the calumet, or peace pipe. They often refer to themselves as People of the Calumet.

Up to my parents' generation the American press portrayed Indians as "savages" and described them as painted-faced nomads living in tepees.

Americans, especially those living near the borders, harbor great resentment and often hatred toward all redmen. They say a whiteman needs 80 acres and the Indian several square miles to feed his family. "The only good Indian is a dead Indian," they proclaim.

These border people encompass many "Jacksonian Democrats" who cling to the position of nineteenth century U. S. President Andrew Jackson, who tried to override the Supreme Court when it recognized the rights of Indians and the terms of the Treaty of Paris.

On rare occasions there have been exchanges, both cultural and trade. The Indian Nation, nevertheless, has managed to keep itself tightly closed to most intrusion from Western civilization.

Some Indians take training in schools and universities both in the United States and Europe. Still, they keep close ties to the Indian Nation and to its way of life.

Yet, the silence was broken fifteen years ago when a prominent Indian was invited to speak to Congress and conduct a lecture tour in the United States.

The man's name was Saugus. He was, to every one's astonishment, a brilliant anthropologist and archaeologist. The American public was expecting a clever redman who could read a trail through a forest or prairie and got, instead, a biting, brilliant scientist who could read paths back through the ages.

Saugus single-handedly destroyed the American myth that Indian culture was still primitive or locked into the "survival civilization" of 200 years ago. Prosperity and two centuries of peace have forged a strong, successful culture that is a mixture of science and respect for the past.

Chicagou, on the other hand the U. S. officials had been eager to emphasize, would almost certainly have become a large and prosperous city if Americans or Europeans had been able to migrate west. Its location is ideal, this place where prairies meet lake. It is the gateway between the large lakes and the Miche Sebe River valley that the Indians till and hunt. Chicagou's inhabitants—I was assured—would have developed a center of culture here even if they had been whites.

Greater writers than I have described the Indian lifestyle and culture of Chicagou. It is the envy of the world; nature come to fruition; man, free and unharassed by war, achieving the new and creative in art, architecture, politics, and psychology. Chicagou holds, they say, a culture untested in the arena of the world for it has been open only selectively to Western influences. A journalist such as myself had possibilities akin to Commodore Perry's opening of Japan in the 1850s, one U. S. State Department official told me.

I wondered, as the forms of Chicagou loomed clearer and closer to the tip of my canoe, how I might find a handle to this assignment. A lead, a good lead, it's all a reporter needs;...the rest will fall in place. It will tell him what to ask and which rocks to look under. A false lead will misguide, distort, and confuse. A competent reporter gives several points of view, but it's always the lead, the first phrase, that is essential.

The test word would be "progress," I decided. The Chicagou Indians do not repudiate it, but neither do they evaluate it with the same weights and measures used by Western civilization.

I did not have to look far for an example of the Indians' dilemma. My sloop had had to anchor off-shore as the peaceful Chicagou River meanders aimlessly, leaving sandbars blocking entry by large vessels. Discussion continued in the councils of Chicagou whether or not to dredge the river. The forces that favored tranquility and acceptance of nature were winning. They argued that if the inhabitants of Chicagou did violence to nature, other forces would pick up where they left off and do the same to them and their way of life.

Chicagou—as is well known—is a center of commerce. Grain, maize, livestock, and hides, as well as iron and copper, are brought to this place to be traded, bartered, and sold. Men and women are selected by families, villages, and tribes to be agents in Chicagou's many markets. Europeans rarely have proved capable of matching skills in the elaborate, ritualistic trading. Only, I was told, when a white person learns to depreciate in his own mind Western money and values, can he or she begin to bargain equally with the Indians of Chicagou.

The water that dripped from my paddle was clear. It was clean and crystalline, reminding me that the Indians, who did not always create progress, were most careful not to lose that which they valued. Not a drop of sewage or waste ever is allowed into Lake Michiganin. The waters are treated as a sister by the Indians, who expend extraordinary energy and ingenuity in disposing of their waste in order not to ruin the lake. They have found ways to dry and then burn sewage in order to provide heat and fertilizer. The village's size was controlled by this priority, as have been its dreams.

The strong language by which the Indians would call this lake a "sister" was foreign to me. I can use words, but I only stammer before their feeling for this lake. Even Indian children have "inherited" it through story and ritual, and all are bonded to Lake Michiganin.

As I slipped across the last sandbar before the dock at the mouth of the river, my mind and body had not slowed enough to meet the pace of the early morning village that confronted me. I wished not to meet Chicagou with my pulse different from its own. Excitement had released adrenalin in my blood, however. My watch was ticking on my wrist, although I am certain I could not have heard it. Still, I felt the timepiece's presence as never before. It was I, not Chicagou, that had a tick and a tock for every second.

Before I put my paddle back in the water, I took the watch from my wrist. I threw it into my satchel. Then, I took the deepest breath of my life. I let it out slowly—very lightly—as though it were my soul. With that act, my body slipped into a different world. I crossed a line which would be to me as decisive as death itself.

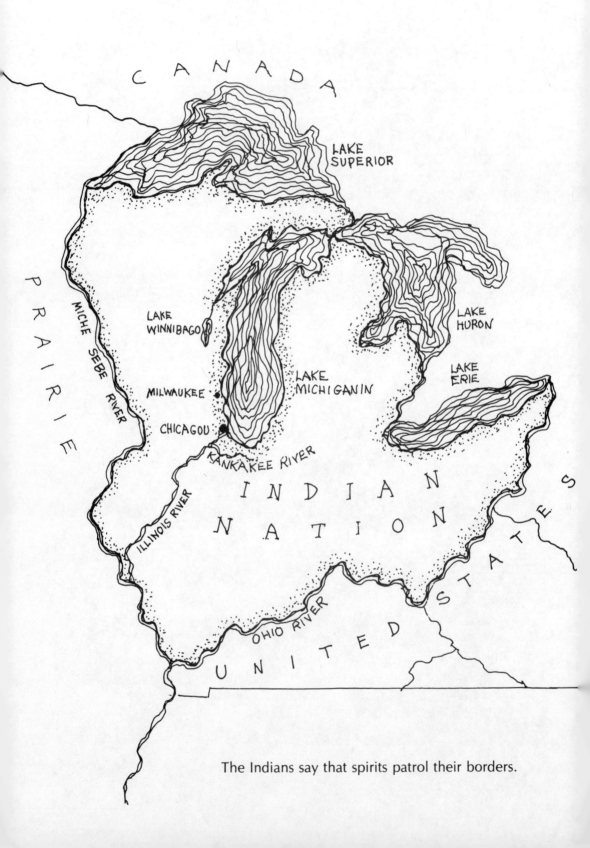

The Indians say that spirits patrol their borders.

Chapter 3

A Council of Three

Chicagou teases the arriving visitor with its size. The village is on a plain along the shore of Lake Michiganin and affords no vantage point from which to judge its extent. Trees and a few windmills reach only slightly above the multiplicity of one-and two-story structures, which continue symmetrically outward from the mouth of the Chicagou River as from the spokes of a wheel. The streets—they are called "paths"—are broad and expansive.

Chicagou's buildings vary from prairie birch-bark domes to modernistic and functional limestone structures that sweep across a full block.

"A village of contrasts," I reflected, reminded by the buildings, dress, language, and simplicity of the people of an era two hundred years earlier when the Indians foraged in the forests and hunted the prairies for sustenance. I also saw signs of prosperity, innovation, and a sophisticated lifestyle in the careful and functional ways of these people.

The colors of the village were soft tans and browns as well as a few greens—early spring shades, more crisp than warm. I viewed the scene as on a jigsaw puzzle, one I would want to reconstruct often and slowly, the better to appreciate its tints and forms.

These impressions remained as I climbed onto the small wharf at Willow Path and the Chicagou River. Welcoming me, as I had been advised, were three elderly Indians, the village's "visitation council." They would renegotiate my right to stay in this land.

This land. It was, at last, beneath my feet. I was on its commercial doorstep, a dock. Still, even this area was as decisively clean as the main street of a small town in Norway, as starkly free of litter as a Buddhist monastery, and as dormantly verdant as a pine forest. I was not prepared for the care and cleanliness of this Indian "village."

The doors of buildings had something missing. It took me a moment to realize what. Then I knew. None had keyholes or places for a lock.

The ground was still hard from the winter. Patches of snow and thin ice covered splotches of ground here and there. The air was still, although I have heard Chicagou called the "windy village," particularly at this spot where the wind was free to whip up the Chicagou River, at whose mouth we stood.

The buildings—and there were a variety—were a mixture of limestone and wood. Often, they were covered with vines and murals, which add to the impression of a forest community.

The Indians who met me were like gnarled trees in a woodland setting. Each was well over 60 years old. Their faces were not enigmatic, as I had imagined they would be, but roughly pleasant. The eyes of the two women and one man glistened, small attentive, and alive. Their hair hung long and white, well down over their shoulders. The countenance of each, swarthy and lined by years of weather, was yet loose, not tight like many older people. Their clothing—the March colors of the village—was embroidered with patterns of various prairie plants and animals. Its material was hide—buffalo, elk, and deer—but it had been treated in such a way that it appeared soft as wool.

Each of the three greeted me with a gesture I was to see often: palms that opened slowly toward me. I would learn the proper response: to put my palms in their open hands. Theirs is a warm greeting, one of trust.

"We want to share with you Chicagou," the woman, obviously the leader of the council, said. "I am Quahquahtan." "My name," added the man, shriveled and older—I guessed in his 80s—"is Penayocat."

"Keenew, Keenew, Keenew," the third member, a woman, almost as old as the man, chanted pleasantly. She smiled, used her hands to cup her face, and then passed them to me as though they still contained the smile from her face.

"Quahquahtan and I, Penayocat, speak your language," the man explained. "Keenew uses only the tongue of our ancestors and our people."

"Tell Keenew I greet her."

"She knows better than we what you are saying, not the words, but the touch of it," Quahquahtan explained.

"I am told that the Indians of Chicagou have a different sense of truth than the whiteman," I responded. "We are concerned with news and facts; you, with history and context. We have newspapers to tell us about the latest events that have occurred; you have stories and ceremonies to tell you of things that happened long ago. Perhaps that is why you say Keenew can hear and understand."

"No one, we believe, has the truth," Quahquahtan answered. "We learn from all. We, too, have daily papers. What you call 'news' is part of them."

"Truth is something we search for," I suggested. "That is why I have come to Chicagou. I want to write my observations so my people can learn from you."

"Yet, as I understand," Quahquahtan pursued, "you have come to write a made-up story. You are to write what might have been if the whiteman had conquered our country and our people. Your people want to conquer us. Would you feed their fantasies? We wonder if this is not a danger."

"I do not believe the Indians of Chicagou fear ideas or fantasies," I replied.

"Do you believe that Keenew understands your words?" Quahquahtan queried. "Our greeting councils always must have one member who does not speak the foreign tongue to help us go beyond quick words."

"I have heard that," I responded. "I also have heard that you are fair."

"Your words are easy," Quahquahtan continued. "Yours is an aggressive people. It is certain of its superiority. What you call civilization wishes to overwhelm us. Your God, your language, your games, your teaching: your people think their ways are better than ours. We three old people—no longer able to work as once we did—in our weakness seek to meet you in your strength."

"You speak bluntly and directly," I answered. "This is not, I was told, the way of Chicagou or of the Indian."

"You have heard correctly," she replied. "I am Quahquahtan, 'the direct old woman.' So I am and so I will always be. I spent time among your people. It was difficult when I returned, but it is easy now that I am old. Our people sometimes are confused by such directness because it is not their way. But when you are old, it is easier."

"You are very open," I said. "That is why I am certain it will be well. In my world, women rarely are allowed to be direct. Western culture approves of a direct man but an indirect woman. But, even in our prejudices, I think we could appreciate 'a direct old woman.'"

Keenew spoke several Indian words, first in a chatter, then by using her hands. Finally, she scratched in the dirt with a stick.

"She says that Quahquahtan is dear to her and that she must be apologizing for herself by now," Penayocat translated. "Quahquahtan," she says, "is a beautiful person with much love. If you returned now, you would have seen our true beauty for having met her."

"Penayocat shortens Keenew's words," Quahquahtan added. "The name of Penayocat is also among them."

"I hope," I asked, "that your comment is not a polite way of saying I am to leave."

There was no answer. I felt a chill. I might not be allowed to stay. I sensed it. Somehow I had to go beyond "right answers." Was I incapable of doing so?

"Quahquahtan," I proceeded, changing the subject, "I digressed from your comments earlier about our civilization feeling superior and being aggressive. That, in a sense, is the idea I am going to explore in my writing. My questions will be: What would Chicagou be like if our civilization rather than yours had flourished here for the last several hundred years? Would we have achieved your accomplishments? Would we have done better? Would we be facing the same challenges? Or, would Chicagou simply be, say, another Boston or Berlin? Might it have generated a culture of its own? Would the whiteman be living side by side with the Indian, respecting his rights, religion, property, and culture? Or would the civilization we call 'Western' now dominate—or even have destroyed—yours?"

"Your questions," Penayocat responded, "can be our future. We live in fear that the whiteman will smash the treaty and recant his promises. He has tried many times but fate has remained on our side. But, if the gate ever opens, no one can go back. Your questions touch our deep fears."

"I believe," I assured him, "that more than fate is on the Indians' side. There seems to be worldwide respect for the Indian culture of the North American continent. And we know, as you do, that the center of that culture is Chicagou."

"Do not be deceived," Quahquahtan cautioned. "We are not filled with such illusions."

"Again," I laughed, "I see what you mean about being a direct old woman."

I now wanted truly to stay in Chicagou. My eyes had been darting past the elderly trio, noticing birds, plants, and architecture—shades and symmetry beyond my imagination. A stop-here feeling with a welcome attached seemed to reach up and down every pathway. If I went far enough down any of them, I felt, I would find spring, and it would offset the chill of lingering winter.

I shut my eyes. Like an uncertain student, I tried hard to will myself a passing grade.

Quahquahtan led us in a little procession to a small field about a block west, into the village. My memory of the place is still dear. Somewhat like our city parks, it differed most by lack of definite boundaries. Trees, shrubbery, and brown grass did not end with four-square boundaries but melted into the landscape of neighboring structures.

Inviting me to sit on the mat near a small waterfall, the three Indians fell easily into a discussion in their native tongue. The words, at first, came slowly but not hesitantly. Their gestures told me they had begun by probing each other for sensitivities and opinions on the matter. Simply on the basis of their tones and the give and take of the discussion, I felt both Quahquahtan and Keenew were for my staying. Penayocat was against. I understood not a word, yet I sensed much. They attempted to conceal nothing.

Early in their discussion, I expected them to vote. I felt I would win, two to one. But that is not the decision-making process the Indians use. I soon realized that they would continue until it was unanimous. I faced an equal chance of winning or losing.

The comparable process in our civilization is the vote of a jury. It is cumbersome, suspenseful, and tedious. You must truly believe in the rights of others to survive it.

"Unless all wheels move, the cart cannot go straight," Quahquahtan at one point turned and commented.

Finally, Penayocat and Keenew had a lengthy dialogue, during which they gestured excitedly. Quahquahtan nodded often in agreement.

She spoke to me: "Penayocat feels you come to us bearing disease. Penayocat is right. Keenew says we are healthy, and we must learn to withstand such strains. Keenew is right."

I started to say something about a recent physical check-up. The words about my health, I realized after a second, were not meant literally.

"You stay," Quahquahtan said abruptly. Her words were not an invitation. They were a decision: a difficult but determined tolerance.

I wondered for a moment if it would be worth it. It is difficult to warm to a place where you are not totally welcome. But a pleasant premonition teased me that Chicagou was a "person" waiting for me. I had no choice but to stay.

A descendant of slaves who had escaped to the Indian
Nation a century ago...

Chapter 4

A Chicagou Wigwam

The Chicagou River forks north and south a half mile in from the lake. Flat boats, 15 feet wide by 30 long, traffic on the waterway. They slip out onto the lake through the river, as it bends south before entering Lake Michiganin. These vessels are, in size, similar to barges, but they are lighter and easier to maneuver. The river is handsomely arched by bridges made of iron and oak. The bottom of each arch is not curved as are European bridges but stepped with parallelograms that give the appearance of a pyramid. Round or curved lines are reserved for ornamentation, a sculpturing that reflects the prairie and its roots.

The boat I was invited to board was much like a Venetian gondola. It easily could have carried a party of ten. It was made, I was told, of cypress wood that did not come from the Chicagou area.

Our trip on the south branch of the river paralleled the lake for about a mile. My senses glowed with the discovery and amazement of that 20-minute trip. For the first time, I felt, I actually had walked into a familiar painting or photograph. Traveling on the river was like adhering to the bare canvas, looking out at paint and picture. Chicagou, since I was a child, always had seemed a one-dimensional picture, as in my third-grade reader. Suddenly, it was an adventurous space, and I was a traveler in it.

The village's architecture has been both imitated and adapted in the work of New York's Wright and Sullivan. But these two worked with far more sophisticated materials than were available to the Indians.

A prairie house here is low and long. Squared off, a mixture of wood and limestone, it sweeps symmetrically and expansively across the level ground. It is rarely a full two stories high but is often bi-level. Many are architectural masterpieces with both a sameness and variety. They use stained or beveled glass that, again, the Indians acquire elsewhere in their tradings.

The commercial structures along the river, Penayocat told me, were for storage of grain, lumber, and other materials such as limestone, hides, and meats in which Chicagou trades. I thought them eminently impractical at first glance since they were only one or two stories high instead of ten like our grain elevators. Only later would I discover the depths that these bins go into the ground.

The boat pulled up to a dock in what visitors, I was later told, call the "Wigwam District." There were four long, flat, one-story structures, with a stained-glass turret in the center. A wigwam, I quickly discovered, is the Indian version of a hotel. Chicagou, because of the Indians who trade and vacation here, has many such buildings. This was a traders' wigwam. Others, perhaps more eminent, were along the lake.

The "lobby" of the wigwam seemed to be simply one large room, furnished with flowers, artifacts, and rugs. The roof was supported by oak beams. There was no second floor, and I could see no private rooms. I pictured all guests—myself included— rolling out a mat and sleeping in a corner, come nightfall.

Penayocat—the elderly man, my greeter—led me to the center of the room where light streamed down from the stained-glass windows, playing on a large, carved wood piece in the floor. It was a door. The two women, Quahquahtan and Keenew, went to join an animated group of people in a corner of the "lobby." As we approached, the floor portal opened and a dark, large, muscular man ascended from it, having walked up a circular staircase. From his features, he obviously was of mixed race, principally Negro, perhaps a descendant of slaves who had escaped to the Indian Nation a century ago.

The man stretched out his palms, smiled, and then startled me with the guttural greeting, "*Guten tag.*"

This really was happening, I had to tell myself. I was in an Indian village, being welcomed by a black man speaking German.

"*Danke,*" I replied. "*Ich kann Deutsch sprechen.*"

"Wait," Penayocat interrupted. "Williams has you confused. He

20

speaks English. Wigwam keepers know their languages. Few speak as many as he does."

"Ah," the brown-robed person in front of me said, giving himself a gentle rap on the head. "Indeed, I confuse you with a structural engineer I was expecting. Penayocat's comments are, as always, generous. A good host does not too quickly make assumptions."

"Mr. Williams," I returned, "it is a pleasure to discover your wigwam. It is beautiful. I too have made false assumptions. Until the floor opened, I thought this room encompassed the entire structure."

"Then you are just off the ship," he laughed.

"Why do you say that? You are right, but what did I say that showed such ignorance of your village?" I asked.

"Very simple, "Williams said. "All the buildings in Chicagou except teepees have levels beneath them. Do you know of any exceptions, Penayocat?"

"No, we do not so build," he said. "Where could we possibly get the energy to heat and cool tall buildings above the ground? We are not a wasteful people, and we are not given unlimited resources to squander in a generation."

"Just a second, please," I asked. "Things are suddenly very different than I thought. This building, you say, does not have just one basement or lower level? It has several?"

"Yes," Williams explained. "This wigwam has five lower levels. The lowest one is for storage."

"Then the sleeping rooms are down below? You get a constant temperature that way?" I asked.

"Perhaps it would be better if I showed you. I assumed people knew that about Chicagou."

"This time," I apologized, "it is I who have proved myself confused. I have heard often about Chicagou's underground city, but I did not think it extended to all the buildings. I somehow pictured it as just one part of the village, I did not realize that it included all the large buildings."

I found myself walking down the circular staircase to the level below. It had no railing and I felt as though I was going to tumble off. What I saw at the bottom were not private rooms but one large one the size of the lobby, with a restaurant, sitting areas, and indoor sports courts. There were also several little shops, all without walls. It gave the feeling of a remote resort.

"What," I asked, "is that tunnel in the wall?"

"That is the subway," the keeper answered.

"You have a subway that comes right into the building?" I questioned.

"Of course," my host answered. "All major paths in Chicagou have subway tunnels for travel and to carry supplies."

"Then I shall have to speculate whether a whiteman's Chicagou would have such subways," I wondered aloud.

"If I might offer a thought," Williams asked, "would not the whiteman be forced to use subways and underground levels in order to conserve energy?"

"I want to think about that question. I am not certain of my civilization's will to save energy for the next generation."

Penayocat touched my arm. He became grave: "We have people among us who work to reconstruct the past. They tell us of a great people 600 years ago on the River Miche Sebe. That place our people call Cahokia. It was almost as large as Chicagou is today, they tell us, but simply used up all sources of energy. It took about 150 years, but it completely died and only the mounds are left."

"Cahokia?" I asked. "The word itself sounds fascinating. Let's see, 600 years ago would have been just before Columbus sailed to the continent. Was Cahokia a link to your present civilization?"

"No and yes. Its way of life died. We have learned much from it," Penayocat answered.

"There are those in our village who can tell you far better than I about the past," Williams added. "You will meet them."

The restaurant, or communal dining area, looked very lively. It had no walls or partitions separating it from the rest of the room. A woman was beating a drum softly, chanting what seemed a pleasantly remembered story. Hand-made artifacts stood as monuments or were hung as ornaments.

The eating area, some distance across the room, had a spaciousness difficult to describe. It was large, 50 by 200 feet, functionally laid out, with no space wasted.

The floor in the center of the room opened, as it had on the first floor, this time because the inkeeper pulled a cord. The stairway led down to an area of small sleeping rooms. Unlike American hotels,

22

there were no long corridors. Rather a maze that forms right angles, curves, and twists. The walls were bright with reproductions of prairies, sunrises, sunsets, and the lake.

I was to remain here overnight and in the morning would move in with an Indian family for the rest of my stay.

My room was the size of a parlor, with a sparsity of furniture: a desk at which a person stood to write, a lamp, a large bed. I set my suitcase on the bed. It all but disappeared. I started to kneel down on the bed to get it and I, too, almost went out of sight.

Williams smiled: "Visitors always are surprised. It is what we call a waterbed."

I lay down and allowed it to relax me. The water in it was slightly cold, enough to make me feel chilled. Williams left.

"The difference between us and the Indian," I thought before I fell asleep, "is that we would not be so stingy with our energy resources. We would find a way to heat the water."

The notes that I kept for myself emphasized one observation over and over again: electricity and other forms of energy were not wasted or used for luxuries. Consequently, I saw very few outlets, fixtures, or power lines. The Indian civilization, without hurry or a too-quick sense of discomfort, eliminates much of the need for artificial power, light, and heat. By comparison to American standards, it seems harsh and austere. But there is a deliberation to it, a choosing, that is rewarding. The resources are there, but they are held in sacred trust.

"What we trade here is the care the earth takes of us."

Chapter 5

The Pit

Tradition, archaeology, and ancestoral beliefs are fermenting sources of the Indian way of life. For them, the past does not lose its reality in the bright sunlight of the present as it does for us. To them the past is not a series of historical scenarios to be put down in text books with dates adjoining, but soul and body experiences that can be relived in a multitude of ways. They use all the paths they can to recycle the past, its images, experiences, and meanings.

Metea and Kolees, her husband, were parents of the family which invited me to stay in their home. Their children, a boy and girl, were Usama and Wapaco. They had a strong sense of family but no last name. Their home, quite spacious, was three miles north, along the lake.

On a stroll the first morning, Metea mentioned a third child, Ojuiba. Others in the family referred to her as an ancestor. But they also mentioned recent contacts with her.

"Who is Ojuiba?" I asked Metea. "Somehow, I sense that I know something about her." A faint breeze touched me as I said her name. I did not share this strange feeling with Metea.

"Ojuiba is the moon to us. It is for you to meet her. You shall."

"Is she your daughter or your ancestor?"

"She is both; two moons in our sky."

"I will meet her?"

"Tomorrow morning. We will journey there."

A curtain hiding a mystery had been lifted by one corner. It refused to go up any farther.

It was a pleasant walk. We talked of much. I told of my family and she spoke of hers. Kolees and Metea, I was surprised to learn, did not have a single job, but several. He was a grain trader and a business statistician, somewhat similar, apparently, to an accountant. Metea was a specialist with retarded children and also worked compiling records for the Chicagou ancestoral councils.

The family was talkative, out-going and highly verbal. Their English was excellent, Metea having been an instructor in the language for many years.

In the afternoon I was invited by Kolees to visit the great grain trading market of Chicagou, the throbbing, exciting heart of Chicagou's business activities. Kolees was a friendly person although not as warm and personable as his wife. With Metea, I quickly forgot she was Indian, but not so with Kolees. Being parents, both seemed to enjoy explaining things to me.

The Indians grow three major crops: wild rice, corn, and wheat. The wild rice is harvested in the rivers, in marshes, and along the banks of thousands of lakes in the Indian Nation. Of the three, wild rice has a special sacredness to it, a crop that the Indians of the area have harvested from canoes for hundreds of years. Some wild rice to-day is garnered with mechanical farm implements, but most of it still is picked by families, gliding quickly and surely through the rice, striking certainly so as not to waste a stalk.

Corn and wheat are grown extensively in the rich "bottom" land along rivers and in vast stretches of borders between woods and prairies. In planting there, Kolees explained, Indians do not destroy the forest by leveling trees, or the prairie by breaking roots. Rather, they have found a buffer zone between the two and use it carefully.

"Let me tell you what can happen if we do not do this," Kolees added. "In an area to the west and north, where a small river enters the Miche Sebe, many generations ago lead was found. The Indians traded it with the whiteman for many needed things. The Indians were taught to melt the lead down. Your people needed it for their cannonballs and bullets, and they strove to make our people greedy."

"I have heard of it," I interrupted. "I believe the place is called Galena."

"The Indians of that area became very rich, and many envied

them. They owned fine things and possessed much money. They had a village on the Bean River, where large boats came up from the Miche Sebe to load ore and deliver goods of the whiteman."

"You speak in the past tense. What happened?"

"The Indians cut down the trees to build fire to melt the lead ore. Finally, they cut down so many trees that their roots no longer held the soil, and the earth flowed into the river."

"Yes?"

"And boats could no longer come up the Bean River from the Miche Sebe. The village is no longer."

"But what has that to do with crops?"

"Almost all of the Indian Nation is on land sloped gently toward the Miche Sebe River. The black earth is held fast by the roots of the trees and the prairie plants. If we misuse it, the land would flow to the river, not as fast as where the ore was mined, but just as surely."

"Ah," I said, "the Indians value the land."

"No, not value, love. The land is brother to our people. We talk to the earth and it talks to us. We care for each other."

As our conversation progressed, Kolees led me into a large room in a wigwam in the center of Chicagou. Here, trading was conducted in rice, corn, and wheat.

We stood on a balcony and watched as traders worked in a sunken area he told me was called "The Pit." They communicated with words, looks, hand signals, and notebooks. While the majority were men, women constituted over a third of this highly-animated group.

"What we trade here," he explained, "is the care the earth takes of us. We work here. The commodities are principally gifts from the earth, the means that one form of life gives to another to survive and flourish."

A commotion in one corner of the large room centered around a middle-aged, somewhat paunchy man who seemed to speak with his fingers. He was walking in small circles, and people were following him around. The scene reminded me of the excitement and animation of a school playground on the first day after vacation.

"But where's the profit motive? What lubricates the wheeling and dealing that must be going on down on the floor of this grain exchange?" I asked.

"Tangible profits—as your economists call them— are not the goal here. Our 'gains' come from caring for people and helping to feed them. That trader in the far corner is the much-honored Kepotah, a hero in our nation. Several days ago, I was talking with him and asked about his day. He told of a 'deal,' as you would call it. For several shiploads of rice and wheat, he had negotiated for a medical library, farm implements, and the stipulation that the French trading company would send one-third of the shipment free to an African tribe. Kepotah does not use currency, even as an intermediary as most Indian traders do. He was handling the grain from three separate villages and would have to negotiate the medical books and farm implements in separate transactions to meet the needs of those villages."

"Then, many do use money ?"

"Yes. It is convenient. Our nation, however, has no true monetary system. Our money is whatever we produce. We will sometimes use other people's coins to help facilitate trades, but we do not have banks. It is because we do not store money."

"Is no one greedy in your world?"

"By your standards, no. The way is lighted by traders such as Kepotah. He is a person who is one with the fields and the workers in them."

"Still, the system seems hard to maintain."

"Internally, it is not. Our people have dug into and explored a site along the Miche Sebe River where 500 generations lived in succession. They lived close to nature and in peace."

"Yes?"

"They lived a few hundred miles south of here. They traded, for we have found shells and tokens from their culture in an old site dug up in the area. They lived in peace and did not create enemies by gleaning much and allowing their neighbors little. How many wars you have had to fight to maintain your system."

"That's an inverted way of looking at capitalism!"

"Inverted? Ojuiba has a wise friend who has experienced your culture, your 'system' as you call it. He said to me once, with a pained face, 'It is as though they do not have philosophers or teachers to help them look at themselves from a distance, to consider what could be. The child who plays and has imagination can enjoy that which might be every bit as much as that which is. The whiteman does not know how to be that child, how to play."

"The man condemns us rather harshly."

"Perhaps. He is in the past. He has much anger from the time when the whiteman drove the Indians from the coastal lands."

"This has something to do with your daughter, who is also an ancestor?"

"Yes."

"What?"

"Tomorrow you will learn."

A messenger handed Kolees a note. He read it and broke out with a smile. He put his arm on my shoulder.

"It is from Kepotah," he said. "He has noticed you and is aware of why you are here. He says that it is not for you to watch the trading but to participate. He asks you to tell him what the whiteman will give for 2,000 bushels of Indian corn. Tell him."

"What? You mean he wants a suggestion from me?"

"No, not a suggestion.He would give you full responsibility. He would not give only the shadow of it. That is not his way."

"He doesn't know me. I might trade him something inappropriate or even stupid."

"Would you?"

"No."

"So. He wants an answer."

"Wait! Let's see. An airplane? An X-ray machine? The great books of Western literature? Tools? Sculpture, art, music? Toys? Hybrid seeds?"

"Your people run quite a general store. That list far exceeds the beads, blankets, and whiskey they used to offer the Indians."

"You taunt me! I am delighted to hear you get sarcastic, even once."

"I do not apologize," he said, with half-twinkle, half-sheepish grin. "So, what should I tell him you'll trade for?"

"Plastics," I wanted to say for some reason, but I just shook my head. I did not have the courage for such a serious game.

"Nature is our sister. She holds our hand while we cross the abyss."

Chapter 6

Metea

Morning surrounded us as Metea and I canoed southward on Lake Michiganin. Nature, brisk and alert, thought it time to play rather than do its chores. Every few minutes a fish would bestir itself out of the water and then plop back in. The breeze carried a slight chill. As the sun reached through slits in the overcast sky, I could see it teasing small splotches of water, creating a hundred thousand tiny, shimmering smiles of gold. Then, as quickly, the sun withdrew and returned the lake to a mass of cold, puckered blue lips.

Metea, in the back of the canoe, glided it firmly and certainly along a line one hundred feet from shore. The cadence of her paddling matched the ease of her voice as she described parts of Chicagou we passed. Telling the story of a people, she believed, is a sacred trust, and she extended it well, I thought, as descriptions and anecdotes evolved into the saga of her tribe.

"Five generations ago," she said, "the center of our village was destroyed by a great fire. It burned for two days, destroying homes, wigwams, and valued relics of our past. People died. Stories are still passed down within families of the terrible devastation and destruction caused by the great Chicagou fire and the effects it had on lives.

"The fire came as the winds and storms do from the southwest. It swirled through our village, though, and ended at the lake. Tremendous flames bared the bones of buildings and curled them into ashes. Our people ran into the water, saving merely themselves.

"Chicagou had grown very fast. It was the core of the Indian Nation. Foreign countries, especially during their wars, had wanted all that Chicagou could produce. And our people had borrowed much knowledge and many ways from yours. We had dug a canal and were being sold a railroad.

"We had grown strong in peace. The Potawatomi, the Miami, the Chippewa, the Ottawa, the Kickapoo, the Sac, and the Fox had smoked the calumet.

"We borrowed from the League of the Iroquois, as did your nation, in forming a government. We believed in our ancestors and in the teachings of Hiawatha.

"But changes came, and they were too great and too fast. The village of Chicagou had grown large. It was not prairie any longer, but a large field with weeds and rocks and trees as well as grasses and flowers that belong to our prairies.

"The fire came. It destroyed what had been built too fast. There were deaths because our buildings had been put together too quickly. These structures served not our people but yours, so they could make a profit.

"Many non-Indian ways were destroyed in that fire, killed off as are intruding trees and bushes when the prairie burns."

"With prosperity, certainly, your ancestors could have easily built up Chicagou after the fire?" I asked.

"No. The way was not easy afterward. The councils were many that were held into the night to find a course. In them, we more easily speak than decide. My people saw in the council fires your vision of progress: 'industrialization' is the word you use!

"The Great Fire had scorched the mixture of our ways. Now, the council fires were used to look into the past and the future. My ancestors saw iron melted into both guns and plowshares in those fires. They saw the explosions in your civilization and the struggle in ours.

"Those council fires, it is said, burned ten years. We invited your people and politicians sent by your President to sit with us often. But, also, we danced with our ancestors and let all, even the most angry, speak.

"Our people could come to no decisions. Their thoughts were as scattered as the lakes in the land of the Fox. The sky did not come down to join them.

"Then, one day, a woman spoke to the council. I told you that all were allowed to talk. That did not include women. According to the League of the Iroquois, we women had certain power but also separate councils.

"The woman was Watseka."

"You speak her name with awe!" I interjected.

"As a little girl, I memorized her speech, as had my mother. These are her words:

" 'Leaders of our people, brothers, fathers, husbands, sons . . .I come here on a day when the clouds are high. The sky is blue. The birds come from the south. Spring is coming to our lives.

" 'Before this day, no woman has spoken at these councils. So it was in the days when the squaw did not throw the spear as far as the brave. So it was when she held the future in her womb or arms while braves wrestled with the present on the battlefield.

" 'Today, there is no war. We—women and men—both hold the present and future in our arms.

" 'I speak to you this day for your sisters, your daughters, your wives . . . and for more. Before I came to this council, we women went out to the prairies, the woods, and the waters. We spoke with our sisters, the plants and the animals, and with our mother, the earth.

" 'And we listened.

" 'We asked them what we should do. And they told us. They said, 'Be free.'

" 'We thought we were, but they repeated, 'Be free.'

" 'We smiled at their message and they laughed back, 'Be free.'

" 'So we learned from their freedom. We lay down in the prairies and let ourselves be as the plants. We blossomed slowly with them. Our bodies could not fly with the birds, but our spirits did.

" 'We have come here today to ask nothing, to demand not a thing. It is we who are free. Women will no longer exercise separate power or sit at different councils. If we do not share the council fires with you, we will have none. We will not walk toward our future in moccasins cast off by men. We throw them away. We are free.

" 'We will not serve and say that it is love.

" 'So speaks the woman, girl, child, plant, and the earth itself.' "

I looked back. Metea had quoted the speech in the soft, firm tones of heroic poetry. Her eyes twinkled with the confidence of her ancestor.

She continued:

"I do not know the words of response, if there were any. I wish I had been there."

"What a powerful alliance the men faced," I exclaimed.

"The alliance became as one among my people. The speech was repeated in its own form in all homes that night. Both mothers and daughters had gone to the prairie and bonded their feelings."

"What a shift!"

"It was as though a logjam on the river broke. One log became free and the others worked loose. We all found our course."

"Is that what freedom meant?"

"Yes. The council members walked the paths the woman had. They went out to the prairies and to the woods and to the dunes. They heard the same message, 'Be free,' and they became so. They gave up obligations to the past and the compulsions of present and future. They held nothing tightly. They saw who they were in history and chose to be themselves. They accepted the past and willed the future."

"Give me an example."

"Leadership. Men had struggled to be chief and then groped with waning strength to hold power. We learned from the plants that strength often comes from bending with the wind. We learned no one can be more or less than he or she is."

"Metea, how could those same ancestors of yours choose a course that shut out my people? If freedom were the answer,why not share it with the whiteman? Why not find a way to bind our destinies? What happened?"

"The World's Columbian Exposition."

"You don't mean that?"

"Yes, I do."

"What had it to do with what we are talking about? Was it some kind of cataclysm that tore our people apart?"

"Yes. Look over there." She pointed to a domed building with two long rectangular wings. It was built in neo-classical style and seemed out of place in the Indian Nation.

"That was part of the Columbian Exposition four generations ago," she said.

"I read about it in my school books. It was in 1893."

"What did you read?"

"That there was a grand world's fair. That people from all around the earth visited the Indian Nation and that your people let the United States government and industry build it here as a good will gesture to celebrate Columbus coming to the New World. It was to be the cornerstone of future cooperation and possibly even the unification of our nations. I saw pictures of imposing white buildings that reminded me of Rome and Greece. I have always thought it was fantastic. Instead, it became the last time unrestricted travel was allowed between our nations. I have no idea why."

"O, young man," Metea said, relaxing her stroke in order to speak with more energy. "Our people recall it so very differently. Your nation proposed it as a cultural beachhead on our shoreline. Our councils accepted in the spirit of openness to your ways.

"Our councils misjudged your nation. They thought you were going to raise up a place that would speak of your form of government, which we respect, of your native art and culture, of your inventiveness, of your machinery and science, of your learning."

"Well?"

"No. Your people did not do that. They built an enormous white city that at first made us want to laugh until we realized that it was actually a white, polluted cloud over our land."

"What?"

"A miasma, swamp gas. You do not understand. The bigness of it. Your people wanted to build enormous council halls, churches, and schools. It was as though beauty to your people existed for the purpose of overawing and intimidating men and women. Do you know what I am saying?"

"I do, and I do not."

"It was the 'white' that was so sad. White is the color your rich people used for their fences and their clothes. I am told they needed servants to keep it so. For us, it is the color of nothing, truly not of life."

"Personally, I like white."

"Yes, that is the notion that went out from the Columbian Exposition and circled the globe: beauty is the big, the awesome, and the absence of the dirt and grubbiness of humanity. It is a color that separates man from the plant and animal worlds.

"Why did your nation give us something so barren? Why did the architects merely imitate the past? Why was there nothing of themselves in that showcase?"

"But why were your people so directly threatened by all this?"

"Your people use the word 'progress' and make it their purpose. It is as though going somewhere, anywhere, and moving—even on a conveyor belt—is your goal. Life speeds up and you have to use things to keep going faster. The Columbian Exposition was full of conveyor belts. A sidewalk was even made of a conveyor belt. We saw ourselves as one item on a long list of what you wanted to use in your unseeing haste. But we had been to the prairie, where growth is slow and natural."

"Metea, we value progress, but it is an upward movement."

"But you must understand. We had learned that movement is not the goal. To be is."

"Did your people see their existence threatened by the World's Columbian Exposition?"

"Yes. You took nature and plants and put them in a musuem ...in that building over there: chloroformed butterflies, stuffed animals, and a taxidermied passenger pigeon. We would have been next. Nature is our sister. She holds our hand while we are crossing the abyss."

I felt jolted. I felt there were flaws in her reasoning, but they were more in context than in fact.

"So," I blurted out, "is the answer simply to turn your back on progress?"

"We believe the issue is not progress but growth. You rape the soil not because your people are hungry, but to make fast, quick profits. You want to take all you can as fast as you can in the name of progress."

"But people are hungry."

"So will our great-great grandchildren be if we abuse the soil, and so would we all be if our ancestors had."

"I do not think farmers are hurting the soil that badly."

"You have much to learn while you are here."

For a while, there was silence. I broke it. "Metea. We have argued. There is a gulf between us. I hope it does not grow wider."

"I do not think it will. We are in this canoe together. We go to the same place. A few more miles and we shall find Ojuiba."

That name. Once again, I felt a touch.

Ojuiba's eyes...rubies brought
out of some mysterious
temple

Chapter 7

Ojuiba

Ojuiba smiled.

She was among twenty people digging an excavation 300 feet from the river bank. Ojuiba, I recognized. Her look, a pleasant expression, reached me on a beam of feeling, rich and stimulating. She was young, perhaps 20, yet her complexion no longer had the sheen of youth.

How can I remember anything other than Ojuiba's eyes? All of her seemed but a setting for them, as though they were rubies brought out of some mysterious temple, protected for centuries by scorpions, worshipped by people long gone, who had kept secret the very mystery of life in two gems that were precious beyond comprehension.

I noticed Ojuiba's eyes first and I remember them last. They focused on mine with an openness and softness that allowed me to look into them even at the several-hundred-foot distance that separated us. I saw life there and I watched it dance.

Her features and skin were fully Indian: a reddish tan, high cheek-boned, a little weathered. Ojuiba's hair was thick, very black, and almost coarse. Tied in pony tails, it hung down over her breasts, contrasting with a very simple, soft brown tunic that looked more natural on her than skin does on a deer. She was small, under five and one-half feet tall, but her body was full and lithe.

Images fall so far short. It was a hypnotic moment, a dream second, a throwback to some experience from a different life. Ojuiba's eyes ignited me as though my life had been an accumulation of dry sticks and kindling logs, and Ojuiba's look was the match that lit the waiting wood.

Two persons are brought together as though from the ends of the earth. There is recognition, openness, trust, excitement, mystery, hope, pleasure.

That moment is eternity, and yet it is not eternal. It is a tenderness above and beyond imagination or planning. It is a soaring of the soul. In that second, there is no before or after, but the memory of it contains both.

I know there are people who do not think such experiences can happen and others who throw away all else in life trying to make them happen. Fate, not man, I believe, creates such moments. Perhaps the flame of this second was so intense because the time would come when I would need the flicker of its memory to light a great, dark void.

As I stood there on the bank of the river seeing Ojuiba for the first time, my heart did not feel that there could ever be a dark or a void again. Loneliness, I was certain, had been rooted forever out of my existence.

My face was flushed; my, mouth, smiling. I felt my own eyes alive and dancing. I was aware of how seldom I look directly into anyone's eyes. Never before had I encountered such a feeling of trust.

Was this love, attraction, or hypnosis? I did not know. It went beyond past experience and defied any label.

Metea, who had been beaching the canoe, looked up and started to point Ojuiba out to me. She noticed what was happening and laughed a short laugh.

"Well," she said.

I tried to say something in response, but couldn't. I shook my head as if to spin off a little of the spell. I tried to walk toward Ojuiba.

My trance lasted but a fleeting moment. A word of caution and of warning might have been uttered to me, I don't remember. I proceeded toward her, entranced by the beacons of Ojuiba's eyes.

The jolt came as the earth disappeared beneath my feet. A strong arm just as quickly coiled firmly around my chest to keep me from falling. My breath was caught short. I was confused, lost between distraction and the reality of what was happening to me.

A large, strong arm, I began to realize, had encircled my body and was still holding me in the air. Suddenly, I began to fear: "Someone—a man, a boyfriend, or a husband—realized how totally I had been enthralled by Ojuiba. He was going to do something to me because of it."

The sin I had almost committed was not that of coveting. It was carelessly intruding on something uninvited. The excavation at my feet was not for construction; it was an archaeological dig. I had taken half a step into a part being worked. I had been stopped from falling into it by the quick response of a man who had sensed what I would do.

"You are clumsy," he muttered.

The arm holding me set me down. I drew a breath, turned, and faced the man to whom it belonged. He was large and unusually muscular. An Indian in his forties, he wore ceremonial paints.

He had a bead vest and a square, almost fearsome face. His body was tense with anger.

"Look, I'm sorry." Somehow, I didn't mean the words. I just could not get upset about my near accident.

"Your apologies," he said in a cold, controlled voice, "are an expression of propriety rather than heart-felt. Do you not understand what you did?"

His words cut deep. I dislike criticism, especially in public. His voice seemed just as superior as his comment.

"Who are you?" I asked, with my own rancor, forgetting that I was in his world, not mine.

"I am Saugus, a man from the past," he replied, letting dignity replace anger in his voice. "I live among the ancestors of my people. I help them probe and distill the old ways. My words show you that I also have been among your people."

So, he was Saugus, the legendary Indian archaeologist!

Still, my anger did not leave me as quickly as his seemed to melt away. We had offended each other. Wise, I knew he was; but a friend, not.

"I have heard your name in my country," I answered, falling back on the sense of propriety that my culture had given me. "It is spoken in our schools with honor. Your lectures before Congress a decade ago are still recalled with respect."

"I apologize to my ancestors for my display of anger," he retorted. "They have taught me better."

That comment gave me an advantage. I had to take it. "Your

41

ancestors were angry people. They knew much violence," I challenged.

"Yes," he shot back, "they were survivors. The Iroquois used guns to push the Hurons west, as they did other tribes. We made war on one another. The great peace—it took a hundred years to work it out— healed wounds and made us a body with one soul. We, who hate violence, love most of all those ancestors who had to survive. They still live among us in our children, and we promise them they shall never see a day of bloody conflict again."

The notion of children being ancestors reverted my attention to Ojuiba. She had walked closer. Her eyes were no less flashing, and her mouth no less sensuous. I noted something else. Her look and eyes were arched slightly upward. I have, all my life, been accustomed to young women's eyes being cast slightly downward.

Metea introduced us, and Ojuiba took my hands and gently caressed them with her palms, showing an openness and friendliness that relaxed and delighted me.

"You are here, Silas Bigelow," Ojuiba said. "I thank Metea, the daughter of my daughters for bringing us together." The warm greeting included the strangest of words to describe a mother.

"The daughter of your daughters!" The words came out as an exclamation rather than a question.

"Did she not tell you," Ojuiba queried, "that I am in the past for a year—I am an ancestor? I lived with people on the great ice, who hunt the elephant with the long tooth."

"That," I asked, "is what you mean by being an ancestor—you study the past?"

"We study nothing," Saugus interjected in a tone far softer than earlier. "That is something you do in your land. We work. We live. We do not have the hybrid hothouses you call 'schools.' We do not study the past, we join it. People, while young like Ojuiba, spend a year in the past, living as an ancestor, sharing their mysteries, and learning from them."

"Do you at least teach? I have come to learn," I responded.

"No," Ojuiba answered. "The teacher is never the equal of the student. We share. I have a small rock-plant that is a million years old. I have sand that shows that the land here was once an island in the great lake. I have a wounded bone of a small animal from long ago. I give these things to you."

"Ojuiba, thank you, Now, I must give you something. I do not yet know what. I will find it, and we will share."

The main excavation was of an ancient oblong house, 55 feet long and 13 feet wide, Ojuiba explained.

"Apparently, it was a ceremonial house used in winter. Saugus says it was built about 500 years ago and possibly rebuilt several times.

"We believe the Illinois Indians, now dead, live here, and we want to learn from them."

Ojuiba was showing me lines in the soil, dark spots that had far more meaning for her than me. Still, she was so totally absorbed in them that what she showed me seemed to come to life

"You said 'live' instead of 'lived,' and yet you said they are dead," I challenged. "Your role must be confusing."

She smiles. "No ," she said, "not so much confusing as part of a mystery."

"Have you found graves around?" I asked. "I understand it has long been an Indian custom to bury artifacts and possessions of the dead."

"We touch no grave," she said.

"What do you find here?"

"Meaning. Myself. My past. My future. And now you."

"Me?"

"I have known you were coming into my life for some time. I welcome you."

I was excited by her words, her invitation, but I also was frightened. There was something between us that had existed before we met. We both knew it.

Again, Ojuiba's eyes reached into my soul. My hand took hers, and there was silence.

Ojuiba was easy, beautiful to be with, like a dear friend long lost. She obtained food and a bottle of cool, dark beverage. We walked downstream to eat this lunch together. The small vessels she brought along as cups were from the site. Both pieces were a buff, earthen color. Each had little handles. They added an earthy taste and lent a rich dimension to our repast. The meal consisted of fish, corn, and berry juice, the same foods consumed five centuries earlier on the same site by the prehistoric people who made the cups. We were drinking from the same vessels they had. Our meal had a sense of mystery and ritual, an exuberance that—along with Ojuiba's presence—excited me about life and existence.

I talked about myself, sharing confidences, asking her about herself and the dig. She was curious about my country, too, and interested in the project that brought me to the Indian Nation.

Ojuiba showed me various stones that had been used as tools by the people who lived in the area five centuries before. There were three kinds: primitive drills, knives, and scrapers.

After awhile we said little.

Metea joined us. Then she and her daughter went off by themselves for a time. When they returned, Ojuiba and I embraced, as would old and dear friends, and then we separated without a word. She slipped an artifact into my hand. It was a small shell with a face on it.

As I stared at it, I saw what I could neither believe nor comprehend. An Illinois Indian, 500 years before, had etched a face on a small marine shell. The eyes were perforations, little points surrounded by circles. The nose was modeled, almost as though it were done in clay. The mouth was turned down in sadness. Tears were etched as small lines below the eyes, coming to a painful point in the middle of the cheek. It was a tiny mask.

The more I looked the more I knew. The face was mine.

"Why do the youngsters switch names every day?"

Chapter 8

A Family and the Indian Art of Love

Love among the Chicagou Indians is an art far different from the whiteman's. Wapaco and Usama, both children, first taught me about it. Wapaco, the boy, was an exuberant 11 or 12 year old. His sister was equally full of life, perhaps two years younger. These children, brother and sister to Ojuiba, occupied center stage in the home of Kolees and Metea. They were small, delicate, but obviously bright children, a little too energetic to want to cuddle in your arms.

I felt it urgent to ask all my questions, to debate and to probe my issues with the parents. I found myself literally talking over the heads of and around the children. Kolees and Metea never showed signs of moving the children off to play by themsleves. Instead, they spoke and acted as though we were all equals in conversation.

My patience did not match that of my hosts. Furthermore, I could not keep Wapaco and Usama's names straight. My embarrassment seemed to expose a petty annoyance I didn't want either adults or children to see, and I struggled to remember their names. Continually, I made errors. Finally, I coached myself that Wapaco sounded like the Spanish word "paco" for little boy. I was certain I had it. Then I heard them calling the little girl "Wapaco." I became doubly discouraged an hour later when I heard the boy use the name "Usama" for his sister.

Stepping back, I decided simply to observe. Were they, for some reason, playing a game or trying to trick me? Were they ridiculing me for having made an initial mistake? I grew further annoyed. I had been with the family four days before a pattern began to emerge. The name switch on every occasion took place just before supper. The children reverted to their original names during the meal and for the rest of the evening.

Finally, hoping that the question would not be an embarrassment to them and the answer one to me, I asked Metea: "Why do the youngsters switch names every day?"

"Oh," she responded, "you heard them doing it? If we have a question of the young ones, we simply ask them. I hope I do not offend, but I think you fear to talk to them. They will help you."

"Wapaco and Usama," I asked with a slight flush, "whichever ones you are, why do you trade names?"

The girl—at the moment, Usama—answered: "It is the sharing. Usama and Wapaco, this is the way our love teaches us." Then she giggled.

Her brother Wapaco came to my rescue with an explanation: "The sharing, you see, is not only trading names. We give each other how we feel. We exchange being happy and sad. I am a girl then. I play with her toys, and I am the youngest of the family. I like that. And she is my brother, and I am happy to have a big brother."

"You mean all children do this?" I asked incredulously.

"Not only the children," Wapaco answered. "Our parents too." And then he and Usama both began to laugh lightly.

"Then, what it is," I mused, "is an elaborate system of role exchange. The psychodramatists would be delighted with this!"

"Be careful with the word 'role,' "Metea interjected. "The words of your tongue are important to me. I help our people learn your language. For you, 'role' is play-acting. It is what a person does on a stage and is like a reflection in the water. That word does not fit here. Somthing real is exchanged, something of the spirit."

"To you," she added, "this may seem part myth, but both myth and reality are highly respected among us. For us, it is the total logic, not what you call the syllogism, that is important."

Later, I myself would be involved in "the sharing," as the Indians call it, and come to understand their difficulty in explaining it.

"Do you mean adults do this?" I probed.

"Of course," her husband answered. "This is the way of our love. Do you have nothing of this among your people? I did not know that."

"No," I answered with a sense of sadness. "Intimate relationships and love are very difficult among my people. Two people can be very sensitive and good, yet not very good at loving each other. It always seems good at the beginning. We have never figured out what goes wrong."

"My breasts ache when you tell me that," Metea sighed. "Love goes away?"

"Yes," I said, "it goes away. People who were once in love become angry, bitter, and abrasive toward each other. Relief often comes only in separation or divorce."

"And what of the children?" Wapaco asked with an abruptness that seemed designed to protect his little sister from such a fate.

"The children survive," I said, trying to reassure him. "They go with one of the parents, and the other gets visiting rights to see them." I could see that my explanation was not very soothing. I ended it.

"You mean people do not share in your land?" Usama asked.

"They do, Usama," I replied. "They try very hard to love, but we don't seem to know how to do it as easily as you do."

"Why not?" she continued.

"I don't know," I answered. "Children are taught to be loved but I guess not how to love. Many people only start learning that after they get married. And, I guess, by then it might be too late."

"You tell us sad things," Kolees said. " The joy of our lives is our love. We fill ourselves with it every day, and it nourishes us. It is painful to know that others thirst for love and do not have it."

"I feel sad, too," I commented. "For there is the belief in our culture that only others are truly happy. The disillusionment comes when we discover that they are no better off than us. Now, I find this way to happiness and loving."

"Oh, we are not completely happy," Metea responded. "Where there is great love, there is great pain. We hurt when we hear of your misfortune. We will suffer, and those with whom we share this will suffer, too. We ache when a neighbor is sick or betrayed. 'Hurt' is like a rock dropped in a very calm pool. The rings spread out very far. We feel much joy and much sorrow, but the greatest pain would be not to have love."

"It is," I said, feeling that I was a case in point. "I will say no more. I do not want to spread pain among so many people."

"You do not understand," Kolees chided me. "That is what we mean by sharing. I would become you and take your pain. And then

49

Metea would become me and assume my sadness. Then my sister would do that for her, and so it continues until the pain and suffering is diluted and replaced by joy and love.''

"That sharing,'' I said, ''seems a little different than what I see Usama and Wapaco doing. Theirs seems more structured and less spontaneous. Is it?''

"Of course,'' Kolees answered. "For children, there are more structures. But we also go back to them. Kolees and Metea share much. She goes where I trade, and I do her work. I use her name and she uses mine. She takes credit for my deeds and blame for my faults and I, for hers. She sings very well, but I am bad. So, we are both happy and sad with our singing.''

"You are beginning to frighten me a little,'' I said, for the first time challenging their concept of sharing. "You don't seem to leave much room for individuality.''

"We do not know what you mean by the word 'individuality,' '' Metea queried. "You say it as though it were something to be defended at the expense of others. We are free people, seemingly freer because we are happy and we love and we share.''

"You touched a sensitive point,'' I replied. "Individuality is used as a defensive word in our culture. People are sent to war in defense of it, though its meaning seems elusive.''

"That's horrible,'' Metea gasped.

"Not entirely,'' I attempted to explain. "The kernel of wisdom in the concept is that we have to protect ourselves and others from surrendering personal responsibility to the state or the group.''

"Actually,'' Metea countered, ''we share it. No one ever loses her or his responsibility. We are equals and therefore there is no one greater to whom to give it. And to steal someone's responsibility would be as wrong as to steal her or his bread.''

"Then,'' I added with a chuckle, as I thought of those who might charge the Indians with a form of communism, "I feel you are innocent on all counts. But I have a question that has been in the back of my mind for a good part of this discussion. Kolees and Metea, don't you ever argue or fight? Don't you have disagreements?''

"Of course, we disagree,'' Kolees offered. Metea is a much more thorough and precise person than I am. To me, it has always been a custom to leave my moccasins wherever I take them off. Metea has a set place for everything. We do pit one habit against the other, but we do not do that with our feelings. I make an effort to put things where they belong. She is not personally hurt if I do not. In our early marriage, we often had to use what you call 'structured' sharing to handle such situations. We still do occasionally. We have no wells of bitterness in our relationship."

Near the end of his comments, I had sighed. I apologized. "I am sorry, but your words are difficult for me. You seem to present such simple solutions to complex problems. We ought to bring you people to our country as marriage counselors. Does this work in love-making?"

"What is 'love-making'?" Kolees asked.

"It is a strange word," Metea responded. "It is the 'bodying' that he means."

"Ah, I see," Kolees said. "You call it love-making."

"We actually have over a hundred words for it," I added.

"We have a few ourselves," Metea offered. "But it is far beyond words."

"Let me ask a question," Kolees interjected. "If you do not have sharing, how do you make 'love' as you call it? If you do not share hearts, how can you share bodies? It is so much intertwined with our sharing of what we feel that is difficult to understand how you do it. Let me be very curious. If you have not known each other's feelings intimately all day, how can you tell when the other wants to share the body?"

"To a large extent," I tried to explain, "it is a guessing game and at times a very awkward and painful one. Do not misunderstand. People in our culture who are in love want to share; we simply are not trained for it from childhood."

"That," Metea said, "is the saddest information you have yet given us. I could see deep hurt and frustration. I have read in your books about such matters, but they remain unreal to me even as you tell me about them."

"Wapaco," I asked, "have you understood what we are talking about?"

"Almost everything," he answered. "Is there a reason I might not?"

"Love-making, or 'bodying' as you call it, is a very difficult thing for the young to understand. I guess that is what I meant," I said almost apologetically.

"I know," his mother laughed. "Your people have something they call 'sex education' for young people. You treat them immaturely and then have to help them catch up quickly by giving them a pile of information."

"Excuse me," I said, "but I've always been in favor of sex education. Why, there are those who consider the whole subject taboo and don't think young people should even get instruction."

"Under those circumstances," Metea offered, "I am certain we would favor even so mechanical a training. But it is so far from the reality we know. Our children are free to learn of bodying."

"That word, 'bodying,' is such a graphic and physical term. I am surprised by it."

"It is well chosen. Our language is careful," Metea responded. "We do not want to feel that sharing is only an emotional or spiritual part of life. Children from an early age learn to feel the sensations and needs of others. We are well trained to be aware of each other's bodies."

"You are making me feel jealous," I answered.

"Let me, then, tell you something that I think will please you," Kolees said, changing the subject. "Someone whom Metea tells me you met and like is coming to visit us tomorrow. It is our ancestor, Ojuiba."

My heartbeat raced. My body seemed to ignite with a steady, tender glow.

"It is your civilization that needs to be defended by guns and bombs, not ours."

Chapter 9

What Does The Whiteman Want?

A colonized Chicagou: what would it be like? That first install-ment! I had to write it. Chicagou would have become a great metropolis if Americans and European descendants had populated all the North American continent. Its location is ideal. Here, the prairie meets the lake, and the gateway opens between the Great Lakes and the Miche Sebe River Valley. The south part of the short Chicagou River, I have been told, flows from a point where 10,000 years ago a much higher Lake Michiganin poured westward over its banks and down toward the Gulf of Mexico. This was a natural place for a canal and, eventually, highways and railroads.

I jotted down my conclusions: "The business community would love a focal point where farmers could bring wheat for shipping and hogs for slaughter. What possible limits could have been put on such a city? The land around Chicagou—some of the richest in the world—is not rocky as is much of the eastern seaboard, nor 'farmed out' as are vast areas of Europe.

"The lake, abundant both in size and freshness, is simply too large even for the most gross of civilizations to pollute or kill.

"The assets of Chicagou are a cornucopia; this is a promised land of milk and honey. The entrepreneur could have become wealthier here than in the goldfields of California or Alaska.

"The only comparison I can make to the probable vastness of Chicagou's wealth is to the abundance of passenger pigeons. Even though those pigeons no longer exist in the United States, there simp-ly are too many for them to be blotted out in the Indian Nation. So it is with Chicagou's resources. We could not possibly squander this enormous supply of natural resources, energy, water, and black soil in 10,000 years."

Such were my beliefs. I penned them as much with the Indians in mind as my readers back home. I was enticed by the argument that the Indian Nation has enough resources, for everyone, possibly forever.

I stood at a chest-high oak desk writing out my thoughts. My hosts had made it clear that I would have only a limited supply of paper in Chicagou, and I found myself writing on the back of sheets for the first time since grade school. Such a shortage, I noted, would not be a problem if Western civilization's belief in consumer wealth had spread here. It was annoying, I felt, unnecessary, especially for me, a guest.

A bird sang loud and clear outside my door. My room was on a level below ground, and that sound startled me. I opened the door and found not a prairie bird but the ox-strong Saugus. Such bird-calls, rather than knocking, were the Chicagou custom.

Saugus stood at the door, strong and silent. His face was ashen. His eyes were pools of sadness. He looked through me.

"Saugus?" I questioned.

"I have come to speak with the man who would fantasize the future of Chicagou."

"Come in." I felt solicitous. He was more than troubled.

"What does the whiteman want? What will he take?"

"I don't understand."

"Before the summer is here, my resources have told me, your armies will invade our lands."

"Are you certain? I don't and I can't accept that."

"They but await an event, an occasion, an excuse. If they cannot get one, they will invent one."

"I don't believe it."

"One plan is that your being here somehow will create a situation."

"That's not true. I swear to God, it is not!"

"I know that you know nothing. I have been told that that itself is part of the plan."

"Wait a minute. You are talking about war, about my nation invading this one. I know it has long been a possibility. But Congress must act on that."

"No, it will be an accomplished fact before your Congress gets the chance. Your President has three or four congressional resolutions he is ready to cite to justify his unilateral action."

"Saugus, how certain are you?"

"Very."

"What are you going to do about it?"

"Nothing."

"Why?"

"The information may have been leaked to stir up anger among my people so they will create the incident."

"What about the rest of the world. I have always felt that they would not tolerate this. They have been a strong check on the United States in the past."

"There is only one nation powerful enough to be a counter-balance against the United States."

"Yes, Russia."

"Russia and the United States have made a deal. The Soviet Union wants to invade the Arab states to its south. The Russians are going into either Iran or Afghanistan in conjunction with the U.S. moving into our lands."

"The comparisons are painful. Parallels between the American Indians and the Arabs in the near East are obvious. Every ounce of idealism left in the world will be splashed away by such acts."

"We do not see this as something new in history."

"What about Germany? It is strong and proud."

"They do not know of it yet, I am told, but they are to be offered the Sudetenland, and England will be free to do whatever it wants with Ireland."

"Will you fight?"

"No. It is your civilization that needs to be defended by guns and bombs, not ours."

"Are you going to let my government control you?"

"No. You will hurt us, attempt to devastate our lands, decimate our people, submerge our culture. We will not be a submissive part of that. You will find our prairie roots tough, and your people will have to work hard to separate any of us from the land. We will resist with invisible weapons as Mahatma Ghandi did in India. It is the only way."

"Saugus, it's so terrible. I don't want this to happen."

"How would you feel if it had happened two hundred years ago, if you were standing in the midst of your hypothesized city right now?"

"I honestly don't know. I don't see how I could justify it."

"We do not understand the greed of your people. Tell me what they want? To satisfy a voracious appetite and use up everything in a generation?"

"Saugus. It is the army and the President who are doing this, not my people."

"Oh!"

"People are basically good. They want simple things. They want to be happy."

"I have spent time among your people. That is what they tell themselves."

"You obviously do not believe it."

"We see the whiteman as devouring as the boll weevil or the locust, and as numerous."

Saugus and I were caught in an encounter with more than words. His was an electric personality that charged the air. In the light of his , overwhelming news, I was trying hard to be receptive. Within me, there was a strong resistor, if not an opposite polarity to his anger. Somehow the situation demanded denial so it would all go away.

"The air, you devour it," he continued. "You take away the plants that create oxygen. You put smoke, chemicals, and radiation in the atmosphere. If only you treated the air as well as the Indian treats his garbage."

"You are preaching at me, Saugus."

"My anger is. Somehow, I really must try to understand how a people gets to the point where they individually and collectively consume everything within reach without a sense of consequences."

"We are spoiled."

"That's a childish explanation. Your nation is invading mine. Is it because it is spoiled?"

"Survival of the fittest?"

"Yes, much of that. But then do not describe your countrymen as

58

good people who want to be happy. Do you know the first thing your people will try to sell us?"

"I think I know. Religion."

"Yes. It has always been so."

"Well, there certainly are a lot of people who abuse religion, but it is one of the truly pacifying elements in my civilization."

"My point is made. They will want to pacify us with it."

"I am a Christian. I do not apologize for that."

"Do you apologize for your citizenship?"

"I will if my nation invades yours."

"That might not be enough."

"Maybe it won't actually happen."

"I ask you to leave Chicagou."

"To return to my country?"

"No. For my own reasons, I want you to go out into the prairie. It is where we find our answers. It might minimize the possibility of the incident involving you. Ojuiba has suggested that she go with you."

"Ojuiba! Ojuiba and I!" I yelled inside myself. To Saugus, I muttered something about believing my nation would find restraint.

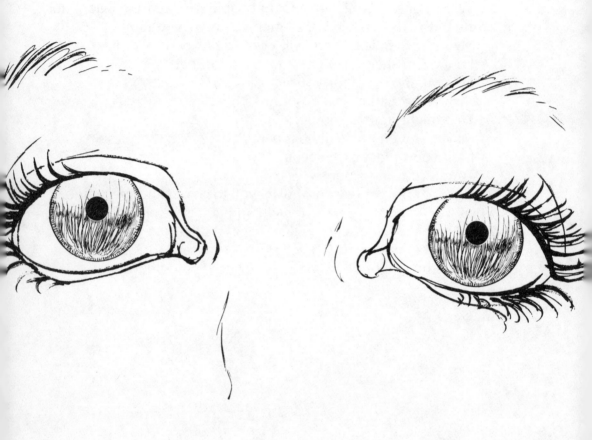

I saw in her eyes the prairie suddenly blossom.

Chapter 10

Two On The Prairie

As a child, I believed in magical places. As an adult, I found one. It was the tall grass prairie of the Indian Nation.

In my youth, a prairie simply meant a small, flat field, specifically one down the block in the old neighborhood where a house had yet to be built. I therefore wasn't expecting much as, accompanied by Ojuiba, I rode in the morning out to a prairie 60 miles southwest of Chicagou. Astride a pair of marvelous horses, we crossed rivers, marshes, wooded areas, and sloughs to reach what seemed an endless field in the middle of nowhere. After we had alighted, Ojuiba shied the animals off.

Saugus had plotted the trip, pairing me with the vibrant, young, and well-instructed Ojuiba. For me, he intended some form of wilderness experience. For her, this seemed an initial test of all he had taught his dearest pupil.

So taken was I with her pleasantness, the excitement of her company, that my mind began to block out the heaviness of Saugus' information.

The prairie, in the middle of which we stood, was not "nowhere." It was the opposite of the barren, trodden little field between houses in the old neighborhood. It was as alive as a drop of water put under a microscope and as spacious as the brightest star-filled night. The experience of it loosened bonds in me that I did not know were there. Its wind-blown plants massaged the tension from me.

"Prairie" is from the French and roughly translates as "meadow" or "field." The tall grass prairies of the Miche Sebe River Valley, however, prove more. They are vast rich lands that flow into the horizon, more endless flower gardens than meadow or fields. We were 200 miles short of reaching the Miche Sebe, but we were, indeed, in its gently sloped valley, having crossed am imperceptible, continental divide just southwest of Chicagou. These prairies extend for hundreds of miles in this area and represent some of the richest and most protected soil in the world.

"Tall grass" is no exaggeration. It was earliest spring, but the remnants of last year's grass still stood four, five, and sometimes six feet high. They had lapped against our legs as we rode through them. Now we stood on the prairie, its sheaves and chest-level plant stalks, thin soldiers against the wind.

The prairie was preparing to burst into life with fabulous colorings. I know that only in retrospect. I was witnessing at the moment the aftermath of winter. Not yet was it "the earth's breast breathing and undulating under the richest and largest of tapestries."

The prairie around me was the form on which that tapestry would soon be woven. Expectant grasses already were reaching up through the soil, contrasting a bright, lively green with the seemingly pale brown and tan hulks of last year's plants.

"Life is about to flood this field in which we stand," Ojuiba said. "These dried grasses and stalks seem columns, like those I saw in a picture of your Parthenon, except here there will be a new flowering."

My eyes rose from the prairie to Ojuiba's.

At this second in time, as I stood there in the middle of the prairie, occurred the most exquisite moment of my life. My past was submerged and, with it, all my tiny imperfections and limitations. The future hung tenuous and mystical. Neither mattered, for the present had caught fire. It happened when I looked into Ojuiba's hazel eyes and saw the reflection of the prairie waving in them. My soul—I then knew I had one—felt Ojuiba and the plants mingle. I often now recreate the image of the prairie reflected in her eyes. The pleasure replenishes me when I feel wasted. I saw, in her eyes, the prairie suddenly blossom.

"You like this?" she asked, breaking the spell.

"What?"

"You like where you are?"

"Yes, very much."

"You have been invited here to meet the plants, animals, and flowers of our world," Ojuiba said. "Hundreds of animals and a thousand plants live here."

"Good!"

"When you came to Chicagou, you received a pair of moccasins in place of your shoes?"

"How did you know?"

"All visitors do."

"Why?"

"Because of our plants."

"Yes?"

"Plants migrate. The bottoms of a person's shoes pick up and carry seeds from his world. These seeds drop off and start whole populations of weeds."

"Weeds?"

"A plant out of place, one out of its community, is a weed. A tree, for example, beautiful elsewhere, comes here to the prairie and struggles to take control."

"Where I come from, we have heard about these meadows. I believe the expression used to describe them, is 'virgin prairies.' I have heard that you burn the prairie to protect them?"

"Yes, it is done. Look. You see no trees on this prairie. They grow by the rivers but not on the open land. We burn this area every three years. Our ancestors did this in their hunts. Lightning also did it for them. Now it is done so prairie flowers and grasses with their roots deep into the ground can more easily win their struggle. Trees—especially the thorny little ones that try so hard—simply cannot survive any sweep of the flames."

"And the fire kills weeds."

"Yes. The birds bring seeds here from other places. The plants try to find a place in the prairies. They do not survive."

"Why must the prairie be a virgin?"

"The prairie is a sister. She loves us and we love her. Understand that. She is betrothed to the sky and to the earth. The people take away her virginity only if they love her more."

"That's poetic, but harsh," I argued.

"It is harsh that man will change a prairie to a field of weeds for personal profit. We are fortunate. The prairie can be restored."

"By fire?" I asked.

"Yes," she said, and her brow furrowed.

"You have a feeling of community with the plants and animals. That is a very simple way of life. It is the child's."

"Listen to me," she said, "and experience the life around us." Ojuiba's face had a brown, almost golden tint. It was richly radiant. There was in it the flush of life and youth. It added a dimension of excitement and pleasure to her words. The tone of her voice was a cloak that wrapped me, as might the garment of a man just made king.

"To us, colors of the prairie are a high sign, a melody like the warbling of a bird to remind us that these fields are special. Plants talk to us through color and motion. Look, then, at the green plants. They contribute as much as we. They store the sun. They refresh the air. They feed the rest of living things. Are we any more important to the earth than they?"

"Nonsense?" I thought. "Plants are more like rocks." But I kept it to myself.

"No, no, no!" she said. "I hear your thoughts. A plant responds to everything. A little extra warmth, dampness, or sunshine, a change in the air breathed by animals: all these touch the life of a blade of grass. And the grass gives off oxygen and affects the animals or humans who pass by."

"Well, I don't know."

"Let me talk to you in your language about the prairie, using your science. Your scientific investigations uncover truth but often lose sight of the family of nature. They leave no room for magic in such relationships."

"Magic!"

"Oh, very much, magic. The prairies have always been the source of my people's health. Your people have come and they have tried this herb or that and it did not cure or did not work. Your people know so much and understand so little."

"But testing is scientific. And that is what is done."

"No. No. Saugus has helped me learn both your people's science and my people's magic. They do not contradict each other."

"What do you mean by magic?"

"Tell me. How does one doctor cure better than another with the same medicine?"

"I don't know."

"I don't either. So I call it magic,"

"Do you say the prairie itself is magic?"

"It is your question. What do your senses tell you? Come lie with me on the prairie. Feel it. Experience it. Listen to it."

I lay next to Ojuiba, with my face close to hers, and looked at her intently. I barely smelled the grass. The ground was cold. I smiled, despite my discomfort. She, however, was more teacher than companion at the moment.

"Dig," she prodded.

"With what?"

"Your hands."

I did. The ground was cold, black, and unbelievably tough. My fingernails encountered roots, wiry grass, and more roots.

I pushed my fingers between them only to encounter more. Finally, I realized I didn't know what I was clawing for and additional effort seemed useless.

"So?" I asked.

"What you have reached," Ojuiba said, "is the prairie's crust. It protects our earth. We honor it. When we break it to till land for corn or wheat, we are cautious. We realize we are opening a mystery. We watch for the unexpected. We are as gentle as we can be, and we apologize to the prairie for our act."

"What does this crust protect?"

"You quit before you learned," Ojuiba said. "You must dig more. You did not know what you were looking for."

"And that was?"

"Look to the sky, to the moon, and to the stars. Is there life there?"

"I don't know."

"And down in the earth?"

"No."

"Wrong!! Under that layer of grass and roots is life. Think what happens to dead plants and leaves."

"They rot."

"Why?"

"They just kind of fall apart and waste away."

"No. Life is there working on them."

"Well, bacteria." I wasn't certain she knew the word.

"Partly right. Bacteria and what you call soil fungi," she said. "If these two quit, life would end. Dead leaves would pile up and not become the food new plants live on." I sensed then how sophisticated Saugus' instruction had been.

"In my world," I countered, "we learn such facts in school. Then we pigeon-hole the information and forget it."

"I wonder if you will not forget it when you write about what these lands would be like if the whiteman had conquered. His conquest would include not only the Indian but also the bird, the animal, the plant, the bacteria and fungi."

"My readers might not understand that point."

"They will if you do. In any place where the prairie has been farmed for a hundred years, the black dirt base has dropped from an average of 16 inches to 6. Do you see?"

"Yes."

"This will also help," she offered. "Saugus gave me this copy of a letter written to your people 100 years ago by Chief Sealth of the Duwanish Tribe. He asked that you read it here on the prairie.

I stood on the gentle stage of the prairie and read:

> The Great Chief in Washington sends word that he wishes to buy our land. How can you buy or sell the sky—the warmth of the land? The idea is strange to us. We do not own the freshness of the air or the sparkle of the water. How can you buy them from us?
>
> Every part of this earth is sacred to my people. Every shiny pine needle, every sandy shore, every mist in the dark woods, every clearing and humming insect is holy to the memory and experience of my people.
>
> We know that the whiteman does not understand our ways. One portion of the land is the same to him as the next, for he is a stranger who comes in the night and takes from the land whatever he needs. The earth is not his brother but his enemy, and his children's birthright is forgotton.

66

There is no quiet place in the whiteman's cities. No place to hear the leaves of spring or the rustle of insect wings. But perhaps because I am savage and do not understand, the clatter seems to insult the ears. And what is there to life if a man cannot hear the lovely cry of the whippoorwill or the arguments of the frogs around the pond at night?

The whites, too, shall pass—perhaps sooner than other tribes. Continue to contaminate your bed, and you will one night suffocate in your own waste. When the buffalo are all slaughtered, the wild horses all tamed, the street corners of the forest heavy with the scent of many men, and the views of the ripe hills blotted by talking wires.

Where is the thicket? Gone. Where is the eagle? Gone. And what is it to say goodbye to the swift and the hunt? The end of living and beginning of survival.

The words of the latter hung poetic and unreal, perhaps because they seemed too much, especially on the prairie with Ojuiba. They were the voice of a man totally out of feel with my world back home. He was attacking it two or three levels above where my concerns and beliefs were. His comments sounded good but idealistic. If I accepted them, I would have to give up my way of life. My only defense was to label them in mind and feelings as "idealistic and unreal."

To get away from my own emotions at the moment, I asked Ojuiba her feelings.

She took a short breath before answering, a reaction that surprised me:

"That is an unusual question in our world," she said. "People here have a way of sensing and knowing how each other feel without asking. I rode in your saddle coming here, but I knew you were not in mine."

"I do not know whether or not to apologize."

"No. Do not apologize. I feel as I have spoken to you. I love my world. I love the thistle on this stalk as I do the birds and my family. But I have not yet learned from the bugs and birds to be carefree. I have fears. I am afraid that though nature creates today billions of these thistles, tomorrow they could be no more."

"Ojuiba, you are afraid?"

"Saugus believes in the future. He tells me my fear is a weakness. I tell you this, Silas, I am afraid."

Ojuiba and I were lying on the ground, looking at each other. We both sensed that we had talked too much. The ground was damp and cold, but I lay silent as did she. We inched closer together. I heard sounds: from the wind, from animals, from insects, and then seemingly, from the earth itself. I heard the dark come upon us as we lay there. I thought of a thousand ways to allay her fears. I said nothing. Finally, I heard—I think I heard—us fall asleep.

"Love is of the earth."

Chapter 11

The Bodying

Ojuiba.

Ojuiba and I. We ran together. I watched her head, her limbs, and her breasts flow with the breeze and her form melt into the crackling scenery of coming spring. She sped at a wild animal's gait, gracefully, with the sensuous, elliptical, cross-over stride of the female runner. The unleashed spirit of Ojuiba bounded through the tall stalks and past the early blossoming grass. With her went a little laugh, as though to say it was all too easy and more than fun.

I trailed her, not as fluid as she. My straight, forward gait did not, could not pick up her rhythm or natural motion, but my body became infected with her laughter.

As we ran, an inner excitement grew in me. I sensed that she, too, shared it.

The air swept into my lungs as no other that I ever had inhaled. I have coughed the pollution of the city and felt the pain of the cold mountain air. The breath of the prairie was the antithesis of both, a refreshing oxygen-rich mixture that treated rather than tormented my lungs.

The air was not merely oxygen. It was also particles of plants. The smells were soft. They teased me with their freshness. I sensed their glory, the excitement, and the budding life of this prairie. No runner is ever more immediately rewarded for every inch he has covered than he who has run through the prairie in spring. The prize is a bursting, sweet refreshment that scintillates nose and throat and lungs and balms them.

The late afternoon sky was a pastel blue, with bright, white, fluffy clouds.

The future was now. It tasted and smelled good. The excitement of the moment was sharply real. My body radiated a soft, satisfying glow of sensual content. We ran until we panted. Then we just stopped and laughed.

I smiled at the new grass and saw a budding flower. I shared something with it, anticipation. I wanted to hold Ojuiba. I wished to embrace her forever.

I held back like a virile charioteer, I held reins on the strong, driving horse of my desires. I sensed—I knew—it was the way.

Ojuiba's skin looked smoother. Her laugh sounded richer. She had broken into a slight sweat. She was a dream, a fantasy.

"I would like to meet your animal brothers and sisters," I said, knowing that I was deliberately diverting myself.

Ojuiba looked into my eyes and replied not with a word but rather with a sensuous, enjoyable, knowing smile. Something in her, too, I sensed, wanted simply to touch me. It was her youth: the freshness of her skin, a lilt of enthusiasm, an innocence in her smile. It could frighten as well as please me. It was a key to knowing her, a genuine dimension, but it was also a fragile characteristic that warned me she could break as well as bend.

At the moment, Ojuiba's youth glowed, but it teased more than scared me. I always had been skittish of younger woman. They didn't know or feel something I did, and that bothered me. But, whatever it was, Ojuiba did know and feel it.

I sensed the touch, the rush of her youth as her fingers reached out to touch mine and her hand to press my palm. She pulled me gently. I did not know where we were going, but I matched her effortless pace.

It was nearly sundown. Eventually, I saw, we were loping toward a stream. Every once in awhile, her free hand tensed and she pointed. Often, I would see what she was indicating, but not always. She saw a fox. I think I saw it. I did see several rabbits, a mouse, and an animal—a large rodent—that she could not identify in English. I could have crossed that prairie ten times by myself and not have seen one of those animals. A person needed her eyes and her pace to be aware of this world.

"Everyone," I called over to her, "should at least once in his life run through this prairie, touching your hand and seeing and feeling your world. It would change my people."

I remember that it was immediately after these words that we saw it. To me, it was beautiful. To Ojuiba, it was ominous. The "it" was a passenger pigeon, a solitary creature on the wing. A bird that flocks in the tens of thousands is uniquely beautiful alone. My companion sensed that this one was an animal in trouble. It was headed south, but then it did a strange thing: it veered southwest. "That," Ojuiba said, "is not a direction birds tend to fly. That is whence the storms come."

"Hey," I laughed at the suddenly somber young woman. "It's a bird. It'll be all right."

"No, it won't" she said. "It will die."

Time seemed to stop, to hang ominously after her prediction.

The fawn saved the moment. Still so young as to be ungainly, it scurried after its mother down an embankment toward a stream several hundred yards away. Both animals were strangely unaware of our presence. Ojuiba's hand pulled me firmly back to a thicket at the top of the bank. It was a place from which we could watch them. The small deer had a tiny, alert head, rather human and childlike. Ojuiba's eyes focused on it, and her expression turned from somber to warm.

The small deer that we watched lap the river water embodied her spirit. It was young, tender, alert, and full of the promise of spring: a carefree child of nature, playful yet intent on what it was doing. The fawn was beautiful, a light tan and white. I wished I could sense Ojuiba's thoughts and feelings as she could mine. I guessed at them; perhaps she thought of enfolding the small deer in her arms; of her own potential motherhood; of what lay ahead for her. Her brow tensed a little, and she seemed to be peering into the future.

No. Ojuiba was in the present and in the past, which she revealed. "I am frightened. I see the fawn, but I also still see the pigeon."

I took her in my arms, I said nothing. My attempt earlier at consoling her now seemed inappropriate. I held her. Even that seemed inadequate, but she responded to it.

We reclined in a half-sitting position. She was in my arms. She began to glow warm. Time left us. My mind skipped through the past.

73

I was back at the dig, seeing her again for the first time. I was on the prairie, melted by her eyes and appearance.

Ojuiba rested in my arms. I felt my own warmth as well as hers.

The reins loosened. Now, feeling sought culmination; but there was no headlong rush. There seemed yet time for communication, for development, even for thought.

Ojuiba was both vibrant woman and frightened girl. She was warm and pulsating. Yet, this woman, this young girl, was an Indian, of a different world and time. She believed that she was living partly in the past, some ten thousand years ago. It did not matter. She was fragile; I felt strong.

"You are deceived," she said, as usual reading my feelings. "You think me weak, vulnerable. My strength, you do not know nor my people's."

"I know your warmth," I said.

"I am not weak. You are strong where you do not know you are. In you are emotions and powers that you someday will uncover." She held me.

"We have talked enough," I answered.

"Yes," she said. She took my hand and placed it against her breasts which she exposed to the feel of my face. They were smooth and excited. They were the prairie, and it was warm there.

We spent the evening, the night, the morning, melting away differences of age, civilization, roles and future. Ojuiba and I were united. We were trustingly one.

I was seeking love, no, excitement, acceptance, fulfillment, and, above all, her. Each feeling, as though a battle, overflowed. More than satisfied.

"What does she seek?" I wondered to myself. "Is it the same for her?"

Ojuiba again picked up my inner thoughts and feelings. Morning was coming and we lay in each other's arms. "I seek," she said, "for love. I know I am going away and you are not. I want my love to be with you. I want it to live in you.

Her words were confounding. I felt awkward and suddenly practical. "We took no precautions," I commented.

"It is not necessary," she said enigmatically.

"It was very good," I said.

"Love is of the earth," she responded, her hazel eyes hypnotizing me.

"Yes," I replied. I had no idea why she had said it or what she meant.

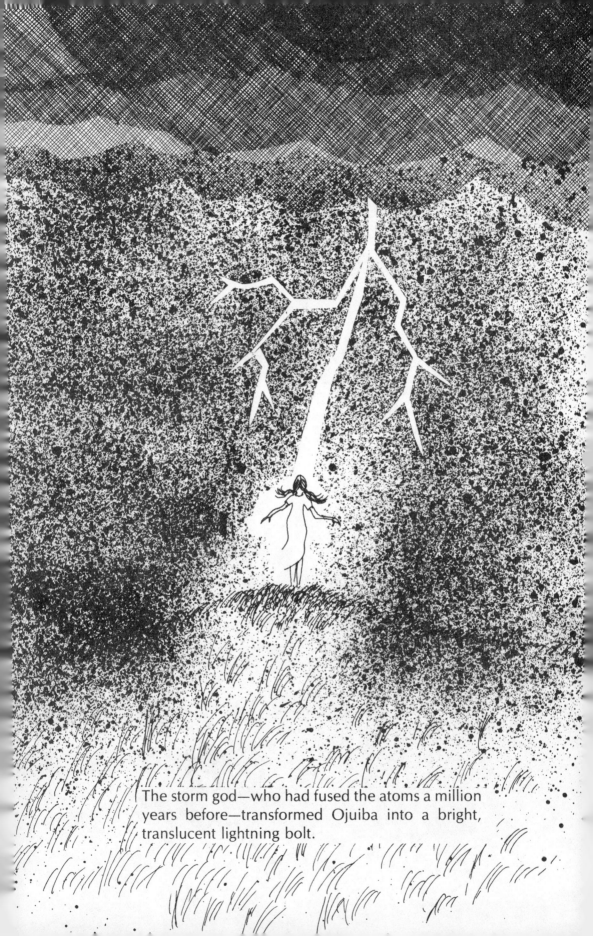

The storm god—who had fused the atoms a million years before—transformed Ojuiba into a bright, translucent lightning bolt.

Chapter 12

The Storm

When I was eight years old, I had watched as my Uncle Edward was sledge-hammered by a heart attack. He had had a little dog, Towser. The suddenness and starkness of his pain and the attack itself scared me into numbness. Caught in that state, I began thinking immediately that his death would mean I would get Towser. For years afterward, I was embarrassed with the thought of that bizarre reaction. Uncle Edward died the next day, leaving Towser, fortunately for my guilt, to his wife. How would I handle tragedy as an adult? Was that selfish little child—the real me—ready to pop out again when I couldn't handle a terrible occurrence?

The storm would answer the question.

Fresh blasts of air warned that the rain was coming. The southwest sky became a stage. An ominous black cloud on the horizon crowded out the blue and quickly became the dominant element in the drama of the prairie. On the open lands, there is no place to hide or cower, no port, no harbor.

The birds—as do all creatures—react to the impending event. Their movements are exaggerated, and they swoop, apparently with air currents, high and low in a circular pattern. Leaves turn and face the direction of the storm. Dry air rushes away to avoid moist wind. Dark clouds grow darker and tumble over each other as though building strength and violence. All moves quickly. Lightning flashes and from far off charges the scene with grandeur and ferocity.

My own body reacted: my heart beat faster and my responses seesawed between fascination and fear. This was a prairie tempest. It was a happening of nature, akin to the hurricane, tornado, and monsoon. It was the fearsome thunderstorm. Dread began winning a foothold in my viscera. The awesome, aggressive cataclysm was growing.

Tiny animals scurried past our feet. The advancing wind pushed them as a great forest fire might. My face was flushed by the storm's moist and chilling breath. I wanted to stay in its path, to partake of its freshness.

Among all, only one animate object seemed to remain peaceful and serene—Ojuiba. She seemed hypnotized, entranced by the display of nature, neither smiling nor frowning. I said nothing. My tenderness had crested in our lovemaking. I felt satisfied. I had what I wanted. I felt separate, disturbed. I saw her Indian features more distinctly. She walked to the crest of the river bank and faced the on-coming storm. Her only concession was to fold her arms to ward off the chill that raced ahead of the storm's main force.

I felt a sudden, biting cold, sharper than any that a sudden drop in temperature could instill. It was accompanied by a sense of fright that changed to fear at the sight of Ojuiba on the hill. I should rush to protect her, to embrace her. I hesitated. "To what end?" I asked myself.

The thunder clapped louder and more terrible each second, a sound as from a strong fist successfully crashing through a wooden table.

I was frightened of the storm, not for Ojuiba but for myself. The thunder rent the air around me and froze me in a block of fear. Lightning cut zigzag patterns of a gold-silver alloy through the cold, black sky. It created instant day when and where it should least exist. The clouds and the rains rushed in a constantly clinking symphonic harmony. Something, someone, had exploded in majestic anger and was repeating its fullest expression.

The force in the sky was driving, eruptive, orgasmic, creating a new ferocity beyond what was expected a few seconds before, as though nature could never again be at peace.

Lightning crashed again and again, each time closer. A bolt struck a hundred yards away. I could not believe it. I was terrorized, my cir-cuits overwhelmed, Suddenly, there was a respite, a moment to get to Ojuiba, to drag her from the hill. I felt, instead a primeval selfishness, just as when I had wanted my uncle's little dog. It was a strong, strange emotion.

Fear, as though a voice, totally convinced me that the next bolt of lightning would strike decisively and that it would hit where Ojuiba stood. The message was a premonition, but painfully certain. I was obsessed with a feeling of death. At all costs, yes, at all costs, I must save myself.

"Rather her than me," I muttered. I was not even shocked by my strange, urgent prayer. I wanted to stay alive at any expense. My feelings, terrifyingly intense and embarrassingly selfish, felt as though I were confronting nature, an angry god. "Yes, not me, her," I repeated. I offered Ojuiba, a sacrifice to my survival. To me, it was fitting. I was more real than she. I was of my people, my civilization, my heritage, and myself.

The storm god— who had fused the atoms a million years before to create life—without hesitation or deliberation reacted brutally. It accepted my offering. He transformed Ojuiba instantly into a bright, translucent lightning bolt. I was momentarily blinded. Still, in the same moment, I watched her silhouetted within the lightning bolt. She was terrifyingly beautiful.

I was knocked down by the thunder that immediately followed the lightning, and I was not certain that the events I saw really happened. I peered toward where Ojuiba had stood and hoped to see her. She was not there.

Perhaps she was safe. Maybe magic had protected her.

Then I saw. She lay crumpled, her body actually smoking. the flashing rain beat down upon her, diffusing the smoke but pelting harshly the enfeebled form the lightning had left.

She was dead.

No, Ojuiba was devastated, not dead. Her body twitched. I held her wrist and sensed a slight pulse.

The toll was heavy, but she was alive. At the moment, I asked nothing more, simply that spark of life.

Before me was the harsh reality of what had happened. I would have to deal with it, simply to get to the pain.

"Ojuiba," I begged, in a shock that prevented me from crying. "Help me."

I remained not miles, but centuries, eras away from help.

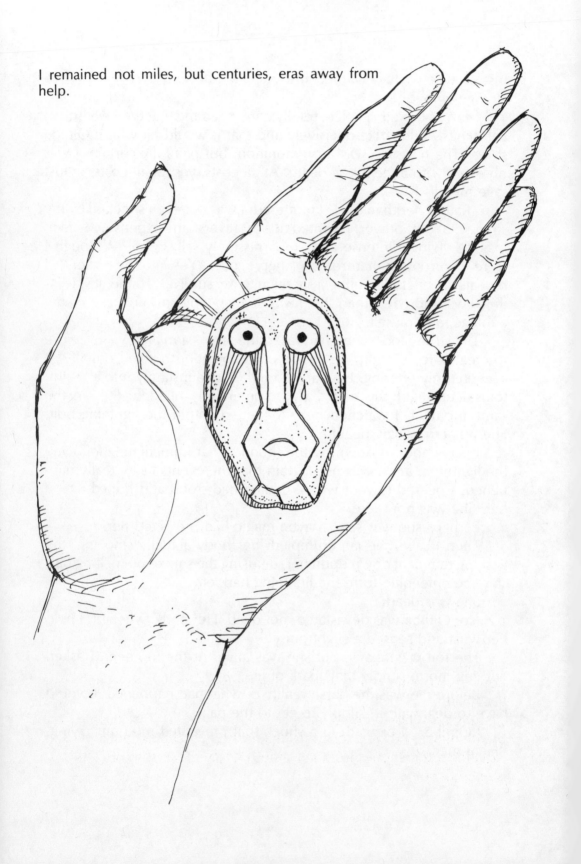

Chapter 13

Keeper of the Fire

The hungry lightning and thunder moved on. The pelting rain did not.

My impulse had been to pick up Ojuiba and race for help, to hope wildly that I would find a hospital, a doctor, or a clinic at the end of my run—or to go on until I did. But which direction and for what distance? I remained centuries, eras away from help.

Ojuiba needed medical treatment to stay alive. I would have to provide what rudimentary help she would get. This was the difficult part—tying myself to responsibility beyond my capacity.

I yanked free my shirt and constructed, as best possible, a tent over the back of my head while I knelt close to Ojuiba's face to protect her from the sheeting rain. Intensely, to the brink of pain, I focused my memory to resurrect any information I might have acquired which now could be useful.

The thought that bounded out of my memory was "shock." It seemed to fit Ojuiba's conditions, and it also was the only condition I had the faintest notion of how to treat. Was my memory accurate? Warmth and "head up" were the two things of which I became increasingly certain. How horrible! I had been careless about learning how to save a life. I later learned that the feet should be elevated, not the head.

Ojuiba's life seemed a flicker, completely in my hands. My breathing was heavy. Hers was an almost imperceptible inhaling and exhaling a few inches from my mouth. How diminished had her existence become!

It was not just a life and an existence. It was Ojuiba. My memories of her strength, her tenderness, her vivaciousness, and her concern for me ran rapidly through my consciousness, abruptly punctuated by the memory of my sacrificial words and the bolt of lightning.

I tried to stem such memories.

Emotions would not let me. Feelings ripped me apart, coming at me from all directions with an intensity that constricted my breathing. They combined, forming impulses toward Ojuiba that rushed at me with excitement and pain and then as quickly subsided, leaving a vacuum of fear and loneliness to await the next onslaught. I felt in awe of this emotional flood. I had not been a person easily ruled by feelings. Now, I felt dominated by a force that my intellect could not control. And the object of that domination seemed the flickering flame of warmth and life that my shirt and body were protecting from the rain.

But a few moments before I had failed miserably in my love for Ojuiba. "Rather her than me," I had prayed. Caught in that moment of naked survival, I had called down her destruction. Still, I had no overwhelming sense of guilt for it. Now I cursed God, not myself.

The rain continued to pelt us, monotonously over quenching the world around us. Time remained illusory. My limbs ached from the huddled, crawling position I held above Ojuiba's limp form. My mind focused sharply on the recollection that a shock victim must be kept warm. I tried to become more a blanket than a tent for Ojuiba. I pressed my body gently against hers. My soul restrained tiring muscles from crushing her already too-soft breathing.

The force of the rain tapping on my body, began to subside. My thoughts moved toward the next step in Ojuiba's survival. I had propped up her head, believing it to be important in treating shock victims. I wrapped my shirt in a bundle and placed it under her head, resting momentarily and withdrawing the body warmth I had attempted to share with her.

Sadness welled up in me, and I felt I would get some relief if I allowed myself to cry. I resisted and was amazed at my strength.

I wanted to call out to Ojuiba.

For the first time in my adult life, or rather in some form of suspension of my existence, my heart chimed out three clear words. I said to Ojuiba, "I love you." I uttered them. I felt, almost instantly, myself choking on them.

I had always known that one day I would express those three words to another human being. It was part of my destiny. I had held them back a number of times when they had started to rush to my lips in an intimate situation. Now, it seemed almost an accident that I had reserved them for this moment with Ojuiba.

The utterance gave me pain, not the joy my heart had expected. My hope for her, in that instant, evaporated. *Ojuiba might die,* she might never respond to me. Even that did not express the depths of my emotion. It was followed by *Ojuiba is going to die.*

I had to look at her face. I had to see it while there was yet life. I had to, if I could, clutch at any sign that she was still alive.

I stared into Ojuiba's eyes. They were the eyes that had first linked us, that had attracted me to her, the focal point of my memory of her. I saw something in Ojuiba's pupils, or did I? I blinked to make certain. Something touched me, deep inside my breast and throat. But what was it? I did not know.

I looked away from Ojuiba. I tried to understand what I had discovered in her eyes. My memory recreated her. This time, however, it started not with her eyes but with her wet, limp shoulders and head. Then it called up her gaunt, rigid face. I focused on her eyes. Slowly, I comprehended the powerful discovery. Ojuiba's eyes had moved. They had followed me. I could not believe it until I looked away.

It meant—and my heart became unbearably large in my body—that I was in communication with Ojuiba and she, with me.

Now, I did not just want to talk to Ojuiba, I wanted to sing to her.

She needed a lie, that all would be well. Or did she?

Ojuiba was almost dead. Only too easily could she reach life's greatest barrier. Could I help her? What could a whiteman tell this Indian woman?

Should I say, "Trust me"?

Stark reality encrusted my thoughts but not my feelings. I fled the inner conflicts, abandoning myself to my emotions and refusing to let myself think.

I felt like crying out one word, Ojuiba's name. I did. "Ojuiba."

I prayed an impossible prayer for us:

"Time, stand still or, more kindly, expand and keep us together in your arms."

We pass, however, not time.

Death and Ojuiba should have been forever strangers.

Chapter 14

Saugus

Saugus!'' I screamed to the galloping figure across the prairie, my shout rocking through my head. "Saugus!" I yelled louder, my emotions vibrating through the limp figure in my arms. "Saugus!" I sobbed to myself, so softly that only the prairie stalks could hear me.

Within seconds, Saugus appeared. He was far bigger than I remembered him, astride a horse that seemed larger than reality. He slipped smoothly off the horse and reached out his hands toward me. I looked into his face and could not believe what I saw. His face was heavy. His eyes vacantly stared through me. Even seeing him through my own blurred eyes, I sensed that he had come because somehow he knew.

"Saugus," I wept. "She is dead." I felt a slight flutter in the night. That is when I believe she died. She lay cuddled still, in my arms.

"She came to me in my dream last night." His untouchable voice choked. "I knew I had to come here. The closer I rode, the more I sensed her death."

I felt sweep across me a painful sense of guilt and shame. So far I had managed to resist it. Now, Saugus stood before me, somewhere between God and father confessor. The feeling exploded in me unchecked.

"Saugus, it was my fault. It was because of me. There was lightning. I called it down. I killed her, Saugus, I chose myself, not her. She was so beautiful, so warm and alive. I said to the powerful forces of nature, 'Better her than me.' I destroyed her."

"No," Saugus blurted out, "Ojuiba is not destroyed. She is with our people, with the ancestors."

Saugus stood tall and erect before me, a man who earned the epithet "noble." Saugus was a melding of emotion, intellect, and animal instinct. I confessed to him my deep, dark personal sin.

"She is dead." It was an argument I uttered in behalf of oppressive reality.

"My feelings for Ojuiba are like the clutch of a storm," he said with sad but tearless eyes. "I saw her interest in you. I let her go with you out on the prairie, certain that there she would reject you and the weakness of your culture."

"I am more easily open to tears," I told Saugus, explaining my wet face. "I think I knew what you did and why. I took it as a challenge. That is what you really meant it to be. If I could not meet it, Ojuiba's attraction would be a mistake for us all."

"I played a game," Saugus responded.

"We did," I answered.

Saugus gently removed her body from my arms. Thinking of me rather than Ojuiba, he took my hand firmly and led me to the river. There, he washed my forehead as though cleansing or baptising me.

The wind was blowing with a light chill. Birds fluttered from one limb to another in the trees that lined the river. The mud was slippery along its bank. The sky was cloudless.

I resented these changes in weather that were so mercurial and that innocently disavowed the violence that had been committed. Better it should show signs of its deeds so I could share my guilt.

My inability to shift blame was more a petty annoyance than a powerful lack. What I felt was a dull, go-nowhere, consuming pain and frustration. It was heavy. It would last, I knew, forever.

Death and Ojuiba should have been forever strangers. I had lost her to death, demon of love and life.

Somehow, Saugus located our horses, and he helped me mount mine. We uttered not a word and set off upstream. He carried Ojuiba's body tenderly as though she were a sleeping child.

The morning air imperceptibly grew warmer and my mind, more errant. I started somehow to become aware of Saugus's feelings. I remembered Ojuiba's comments about how she had "ridden in my saddle" along the same route. I began to become Saugus, and I did not resist. I felt hurt that I, Saugus, also had lost Ojuiba. I sat taller, despite the weight of the responsibility that earlier had consumed me.

I had strange, confused emotions—strong, flooding ones; but, they were somebody else's inside me.

"Ojuiba," I said her name as he might have. I, Saugus, wept.

I knew the moment she was placed in the ground.

Chapter 15

Ritual

The sadness, the reality of Ojuiba's death came in spurts, power-ful and immobilizing but then relenting enough for me to carry on my existence. My arms held a vacuum that strained the same muscles that had held her through the night. My eyes saw a blank vision. My heart felt the thrust of a dull, thick knife.

What might have been now would not be. If it had been a cliff off which she had fallen, I could have jumped after her. My role in her death was as blurred as she herself now seemed.

I was back in Chicagou. I burned to do something. I walked. The day before had been sunny and surprisingly warm. With the rain, it had brought more of spring. Flowers were straightening their heads. The trees had rich fat buds that were popping open. The grass was pushing aside the dead clutter from the year before.

The air was scented, and the birds were cheerful. Action, the pro-cess of life, was visible as the sun gave power to the plants to draw the water upward and become ever greener and taller.

The people of Chicagou were on the paths, coming and going. Several had green paint that they were dabbing into light tans and browns on the walls and edifices of the village. They nodded to me. Many touched me. It was the soft touch of people sensitive to the tragedy I had been through.

How could spring come without her? How dare it start to appear one day after Ojuiba had departed. Nature was cruel, hidden in the soft deception of spring's promises. As a promise of immortality, spring seemed a lie. The grass that has died is not the new stalk of spring. I could understand now belief in reincarnation after seeing this season of hope, year after year. I myself looked into faces, especially of the young, for Ojuiba.

I found Ojuiba in one face. It was that of her mother, Metea, greeting me with a soft look and open hands. I put my hands into hers and let her hold them. I breathed heavily as I saw Ojuiba's eyes in hers. It was only a reflection, not the on-fire look of the woman I had lost.

I held Metea's hands and recalled her comments about death in Chicagou, that it was a ripple of pain and sadness that circled outward as ringlets do after a boulder has been dropped in water. But, now, no comparison could describe the intensity or the parameters of the loss of this woman's daughter, either for her or for me. Analogies are so weak I wondered how people dare make them at the time of death. I could merely let my hands writhe in Metea's and sense the feelings that came to me through them.

Metea spoke: "We have counciled. We ask that you be Ojuiba."

I did not question this confusing request. Words choked in my throat, and any explanation given or received would demand more focusing of my attention than I was capable of. I knew it would be right. I replied, "Yes."

"Come," she said. She led me to a small bark hut with an open window. Inside, it was dark and it took moments for my eyes to focus. There, in the southwest corner on a mat, lay the body of Ojuiba. She wore primitively-made clothes of animal skins. Next to her was a bundle of small objects I could not distinguish.

I closed my eyes and opened them again in one last effort to change reality. Still, she lay there lifeless, smaller, it seemed, than I had remembered her.

"Ojuiba," someone called. It was a child's voice, her little sister's. She reached to touch not the dead body, but me.

It was the "sharing" I thought, and I am somehow, to her, Ojuiba. I smiled at Usama.

People I did not know came up to me and touched my hands and lips. Two gave me objects, one a purse and the other, a very delicate fossil. Both said they were returning the items and thanked me for letting each use them. These were now to be returned to earth by burial with Ojuiba.

Food had been brought, and everyone encouraged me to eat. It was difficult, but I did.

The more the role unfolded, the greater my curiosity as to: Why me? Why not her sister or brother or Saugus or a relative? I asked no questions. Even asking them mentally, I felt, was a violation.

The burial, I was told, would be at high noon of the next day. I would stay with the body through the night. Many people came and went. No one showed sadness or consoled. Tears and sadness were for private moments, but I could sense that the mourners were no less intense.

Later, I would learn that all, including the custom of asking a non-relative to represent the dead person, were ancient Potawatomi burial rites. Each act and procedure had a long history and was meticulously observed, particularly in the case where the dead person was in her or his ancestral year.

I stayed the night and my guests—for that's how they acted—stopped coming only late at night. I saw but one tear. It belonged to the old man Penayocat, who had opposed my entry into Chicagou. He touched my heart and held his fingers on my lips. At first, I clenched them tightly and then softly, as she might have. He was related to Ojuiba, I learned, the eldest living member of the clan.

Left by myself in the night, my thoughts turned to Ojuiba, and I reexperienced the love we had shared on the prairie and her abandonment to it, a trust in me that she had finally allowed herself. I sensed how she had felt. I recalled her foreboding and her fear for the lone passenger pigeon. Was it the vision sacred to the Indian or was it the dream of a whiteman who had not slept for two nights—or was it both?

I focused on the passenger pigeon flying southwest. I was sad. I knew her fear for its solitary flight. Was I asleep? I actually saw the passenger pigeon. I saw the sky darkening in the distance. Once again, I had the strange sensation of not being myself. Now, I felt Ojuiba in me. I knew as the storm came I would await it. I could not leave the knoll.

The feeling of being Ojuiba was expanding and exhilarating. I went back into history with the Indians, as she could, and I identified with the ancestors.

I saw myself crossing what I knew was the Bering Strait when the ocean was much lower. I saw the behemoth. I ate the bear. I felt great danger and adventure, driven over treks by instincts no less strong than those of the migrating bird.

I lived in and off the forest, kin to the animal, grateful to every aspect of nature for what it gave me or kept in store in case of need, I saw plants I had never seen before and animals I could not identify.

I buried a man, putting artifacts and shells in the shallow grave with him. I held one back. I looked at it. It was the sculptured shell Ojuiba had given me from the dig. It bore my face and actual tears were coming from its eyes.

Indian I then became, fighting Indian, as the whiteman pushed westward. But I held also in my hand the calumet, the peace pipe bond that put aside war.

I changed into a mother birthing a baby in the woods, calling upon the sacred animals to protect it and be its totems. I chanted a song that had never been part of me and that I had never heard before. I knew it to be a medicinal prayer. How I knew, I did not know.

This was no dream, but a vision. I sensed myself a woman. I was Ojuiba. I lost my identity as a whiteman. I tried at one point to see if I could recover it. It was not available.

Morning happened and more people came. They were different. The last edge of strangeness was gone. It was as though I recognized faces. I remained Ojuiba, and my reactions were hers.

At noon, Ojuiba's body was lifted out through a window by pallbearers and taken to the burial grounds. I did not go along. I knew the moment when it was placed in the small, above ground burial house of the Potawatomi. For, then, I was no longer Ojuiba. I was again Si Bigelow.

"We smoke with you the calumet. Into war or away from it we will follow you."

Chapter 16

The Calumet

We have received the ultimatum," Saugus spoke, clutching the paper tightly in his hand.

"Yes?"

"It is to hand you over."

"What?"

"As a prisoner."

"Saugus, what are you saying?"

"You have been indicted for stealing your country's defense plans and giving them to us."

"No! No! No!"

"Also, you cannot go back to defend yourself," Saugus said, gripping my hand. "They are going to kill you. It will be neater that way. We are aware of this, and they know it and are using it. They know we will never give you to them to be killed or even tried. And if we don't, they will invade. That is the trap, with you as the bait. Your government is going to catch us in our honor. We made an inquiry through Canada and have been told your government officially denies everything, including the indictment."

"Saugus, this is beyond my belief and imagination."

"Your people have grown desperate for our lands. They see you as but an unwitting war casualty."

"Is the trap actually that complete?"

"Yes."

I thought of Ojuiba. Through her I already had died. Saugus's bizarre message tied into her death, and I felt an unexpected and strange calmness in the vortex of the cataclysm.

"Saugus, perhaps it is simply shock. I do not fear death. It seems to be because of Ojuiba."

"Your government is committed to the invasion. We can resist only with our soul. Not with our lives."

"It is as though Ojuiba has been the first, and I killed her."

"Yes and no. I tried to create her from the past, as once my people put together medicine bundles to ward off evil. I believed, and I taught her to trust in her own magic. Together, we felt we could extend it to you. It did not work. You have been touched. I know that. She knew that. We did not think about the medicine bundle itself. It has been buried."

"But the evil is to come."

"Not as fully as you may fear. As much as your nation depreciates one human being's life, so we respect it. The Indian will lose the battle that the whiteman is initiating. We shall win the one we are starting."

"That sounds like philosphy in the face of a smouldering cannon. Part of me is repelled at it."

"You still have lessons to learn, Silas Bigelow. Before sunset we shall smoke the calumet."

That afternoon I spent in Saugus's library. It was comforting to be back among books. I realized how very different, unfamiliar was this world that I had come to accept. The worst aspect of my own at the moment might have touched me if it were familiar. One of the best did: a good book. I pulled from the shelf a biography of Mahatma Ghandi. It was well worn. I paged through it. When Saugus came for me, I thought of two races on opposite sides of the world who shared the name "Indian" as well as an ability to confront an oppressor without force.

"They are going to kill you. It will be neater that way." The words Saugus had uttered darted in and out of my head. I voiced them to myself. No sense of reality came with them. I could not realize that the "they" was my own government. I had lived in a world where you did not, dared not, put a tack on a person's chair or twist an arm too hard. People from that same world wanted to kill me.

The things around me. The book in my hand. Chicagou. Its people. All were more real than my thoughts. I had just been through Ojuiba's death. My own destruction, apparently programmed by some branch of the government, seemed to refer to someone else. I needed something to look forward to as a distraction. I found it in the smoking of the calumet.

Indian ceremonials evolve slowly. Combining nature, dance, music, history, story telling, and legend, they are pantomime and prayer. While these rituals seem to act out as but foggy fantasies, they are not. They are decisive happenings. In them bonds are tied or broken, emotions are vehemently felt, and commitments are forged.

For those Indians of the Lake Michiganin region who call themselves "The People of the Calumet," symbol and ceremony have a meaning I will try to describe.

The calumet is known to the whiteman as the "peace pipe," but it also has been called a "war pipe." Far more than either, the instrument is an altar for the ancient Indian religious beliefs and practices. It is sacred in itself.

All the people whom I had come to know in Chicagou were in the little park where once the welcoming council had voted on me. Its three members were there as were Williams, the black innkeeper, Kolees, Metea, their children, Kepotah, the barterer, and Saugus. Several persons, friends of Ojuiba, also were present.

The face of each in the group was painted with various strokes and symbols. Mostly, it was greasy make-up. The effect was startling. As with a mask, the personality of the individual wearing ceremonial paint seems to change. I understood why Indians in earlier times wore warpaint to prepare themselves for battle. These facial colorings added intensity and solemnity to each wearer's demeanor.

Still, the friendliness of the people, who sat in a large circle, shone through their paints. I felt a bonding, or as though with intensely close friends. My past felt cut off, both by what I had experienced and by the U.S. ultimatum, I needed these people.

As the ceremony unfolded, the calumet more than I proved the center of it. The pipe had a wooden shaft 18 inches long, 2 inches broad, and 1/2 inch thick. Animal, bird, and mystical symbols were carved and painted on it. The bowl was made from red clay. The tobacco in it was very dry.

Keenew, the welcoming council member who could not speak English, was the eldest. She initiated the ceremonies, chanting a song that had a melody, wistful and eerie. I had heard the Indian hymns at the funeral. This was a totally different music, sung in different chords and cadences from any I had ever heard. At first, it seemed a plaintive whine, but its sophistication slowly captured me. Like truly great music, it was a mixture of the simple and the complex, of emotion and the arithmetic of a metered unfolding. The song that Keenew chanted encompassed me. It had a life of its own. She circled around me and the whole group, dancing as she sang.

"She sings the calumet," a voice explained in a hushed tone. I wasn't certain who had said it. None moved. No one looked at me to acknowledge the explanation or to see if I had heard.

As Keenew danced, she held the calumet in her hands. First, she held it toward the setting sun. Her hands took the pipe and pointed it east and then west. She thrust it hard into the ground and then danced around it, continuing to sing. Keenew pulled the pipe out and circled it in a complete arc, a gesture that included the whole world in her emphasis.

She laid the calumet aside and came to me, touching my face as she had when I first came to Chicagou. She did more. She started to rub my face, my arms, my chest, my body, and my legs. Then she rubbed her own body, giving me a very physical sense of welcome.

The elderly but excited Keenew started chattering, giving a speech. I could not translate a word, but I understood the sense of all she said, as I had when she first greeted me in Chicagou. She wanted to embrace me totally as her son. She was happy to have me as her child, her friend, and her ally. Keenew was a mother with a mother's compassion for the whole world.

Finally, using a flint, Keenew attempted to light the tobacco in the calumet. She fumbled. It simply did not work. Timidly, I offered a match and it was quickly accepted. She puffed deeply on the pipe and startled me by blowing smoke in my face. I coughed and was uncomfortable at this ritualistic form of welcome and acceptance.

All of the others followed the same rites. The chant each time was haunting, and the Song of the Calumet became evermore beautiful. The dancing, clearly symbolic, was exaggerated in gesture and at times frenzied.

Metea was certainly the most poetic. In her I saw her daughter as I never had before. As she danced in circles, I again saw the floating, dancing body of Ojuiba on the prairie. My whole body relaxed. I felt the joy of her presence rather than the pain of her absence.

"We smoke with you the calumet," Metea said. "We sing its song. It is our linking, our sacred bond. You are our son, our brother, our flesh. All happiness to you all the moments of your life. Into war or away from it, we would follow you. For no reason will we war with you. Our ancestors say the sun gave the calumet to Panys and that it was passed thereafter from village to village. Our people are one in it. We are the people of the calumet."

Metea blew her smoke in my face, waited a second and did it lightly a second time. A slight nod between us affirmed that the repetition was the shared smoke of Ojuiba.

If I quoted every word of every speech ever made, I would fall far short of what was said that evening. Never could I have believed that communication could be so vehement through a song in another tongue, through a dance that bordered on pantomime, and through a gesture so strange as having smoke blown in my face. I sat stunned, watching a stilted, self-conscious, individualistic form leave my body. I began to merge into the profoundly aware, deeply democratic group of Indians who were holding me warmly against their bodies.

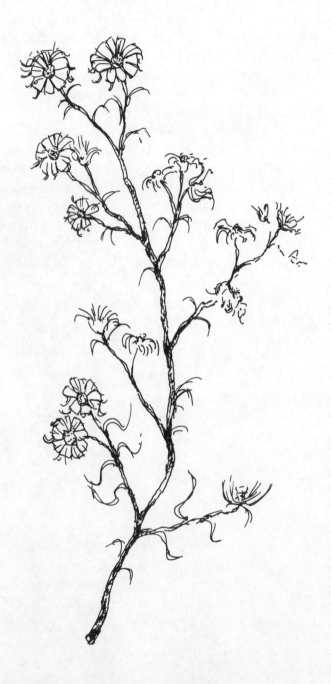

Ojuiba blossomed here and is yet a flower in existence.

Chapter 17

A Dead Flower Speaks

The breast of the prairie was throbbing lightly with spring. The greens were pushing upward through the browns and tans. Long grass stalks, the color of hay, lay flattened and swirled, showing the paths of past, strong torrents of rain and wind. They are a yellowish brown, the brightest of any color in the scene before me.

I also was throbbing. Emotion had torrented through me as the rains had through the tall-grass prairie. My eyes burned from tears that had gushed over and around them when I had awakened in the night with the hurting reality of all that had happened.

Ojuiba I had loved, brief and imperfect as my feeling had proven. Still, a door had unlocked to tenderness. Her loveliness had been real, as had been bodying with her upon the bed of the prairie. She had trusted me. And I, her.

Now, there was only I, and the empty bed.

How after a death, does a person, long into a relationship, ever return to the lonely bed in which the two have talked, nestled, and made love? The painful question smashed me back on my own feelings of aloneness.

The ceremonies and the vision had helped. I had been Ojuiba, and that had changed everything, but not everything. I could not return to the United States. I was not who I had been. Nothing could feel right about going back to a life where emotions came from hoping for a few more dollars or a few more meaningless objects.

That world of abundance and waste! Would not the unfairness of its system, having viewed it from the outside, force me to violence?

The Indians had not given me the needed measure of their tolerance, their acceptance. Ojuiba, with her eagerness and readiness, had retained a passivity I could now merely envy. I felt jealous of Ojuiba. This pain, this explosion within my heart and head, was too much. Better, oh far better, had I been struck by the lightning.

Restless, I sat on the prairie—sharing its cool dampness, a person with a past too hurtful to dwell on and a future without hope. I could try only to be passive and let the present expand to engulf both past and future, swallowing them as a shark might gulp down a school of brill.

Time could be ignored, but it really could not. I could not stuff it in a bag as I had my watch when I came to Chicagou. The prairie around me, changing from second to second, would not allow it. Change was happening in a cadence that is time.

"Stop," my mind shouted at the prairie. "Don't be relentless."

"Ojuiba," I then whispered to it in apology.

I heard a whippoorwill. It was excited. A little repetitious, but animated. I wanted and needed such a distraction.

The scene before me was one principally of browns, tans, and yellows. Some parts were on their way to green but most represented the dead remnant of the past year. Life and death, it was a changing mixture. Grasses were trying a dozen ways to sneak through on their way to dominance. Some bushes had fluffy, greenish-yellow buds in the middle of a new generation-explosion. Moss, a rich green, lay closest of all to the ground. Clumps of green grass reached upward in a bragging way that chirped, "We are going to be green and very tall. We want you to know about our future."

If I sat long enough, spring would come, bloom, and drown in the vast sea of the tall grass prairie's colors. The death that was winter would go away.

Nature can have a touch of humor. I went looking for it in my attempt to think "prairie" rather than "Ojuiba."

I heard the green plants laughing the excitement of youth, the joy of something whose time was to be. I watched a chipmunk scurry out of a hole. Nothing in the wild can be more childlike than the rush of a little animal with the head-down, forward-I-go attitude of the too tiny racer. Had I really seen it? I asked myself with a laugh.

A laugh! It had been a long time since I had laughed. It was necessary. I felt it to be an accident. I would not laugh again.

Yes, I would laugh again. I needed only to find the right path away from my pain. What had I done? How had I tricked my emotions into separation from the hurt and absence of my dead love?

The prairie, that had been the key. I had paid attention to *it* rather than to myself.

The sky was light blue; the sun, not very bright; the mid-afternoon, lightly chilled.

I sniffed the breeze. Spring was in it. Early flowers far off were sending their lure to bees and other insects that might come to visit. There was a light smell, a subtle perfume, as the prairie merely warmed-up for what would in the coming weeks be its grand show.

The earth was still wet from the rains. I remembered Ojuiba's exhortation to dig. Without further thought, I found my fingers struggling down into the ground. The wet mud into which my hands pushed seemed more clay than the rich earth it had been days before. I found tiny roots as well as big ones, all vying for territory in which to seek nourishment. I pulled my fingers up, and there clutched in them was an earthworm, small and alive. A fellow creature. Ugly and despised, the earthworm nourishes the earth and feeds birds with its life.

Hours and hours I sat there watching the prairie's stillness and movements. The insects, the wind, the plants, the wetness, the sky, the sun, the earth. I saw them individually. I saw them as one. The more I saw them, the less I was aware of myself.

Spring was coming to this prairie—no, it was here. Life existed on the surface. It was in the air and below the ground. The winter sleep was over. The action was unfolding.

I picked up a weed—not a weed. It was a dead stalk from the year before, or possibly the year before that. The plant had been a flower. It was a dull gray now. The blooms at the top of the stalks were dry, hardened, now forever mummified.

"This was a beautiful flower," I said out loud, why I don't know. All the restlessness in my soul conspired against appreciating a withered blossom.

I looked again at it. I felt it rough and coarse. This was a flower, I thought. Emphatically, it *is* one, I told myself.

The words of Chief Sealth came to me: "There is no quiet place in the whiteman's cities. No place in the leaves of spring or the rustle of insect wings."

The dead stalk of last year's flower was talking. If only I could hear. *It was Ojuiba!*

I said a prayer. I, who had prayed Ojuiba dead by addressing nature, stood before the prairie now, not terrorized but supplicant, in need of an inner miracle to hear the voice of a dead plant.

"Hear me," I pleaded. "Ojuiba, help, please."

The wind touched me and then went away, taking with it all animation—even my heartbeat. I felt slowness. I was decelerating almost to a standstill.

I entered a world where time was measured by the opening of a bud or the greening of a blade of grass. I shared its consciousness.

This other world was jabbering, everything in it chattering away in the crowd. The plants were talking to the sky and the roots to the ground. The spider was a siren calling an insect. But to me, these noises were distractions. I needed to hear the dead flower in my hand.

My soul slowed down even further. Night came and more than one morning. My humanity lost almost all motion. Then I began to hear the dead plant.

It said: "Life is gone, existence is not." The voice was Ojuiba's.

"A flower, magnificent in its past, is still a reality. Unique as ever. One with its total history: a seed, a bud, a tendril, a plant, dead. It can, it will nourish the future."

"The great and exciting reality of me has been not my life but my existence. Alive, I exalted in my own being. Dead, I will serve others until every part of my whole disintegrates.

"I am no weed. I thrive and belong here, both in life and in death, one with the earth, plants, animals, and air of this tall-grass prairie: each pledged to one another both in life and death. Together, we are the prairie. Without each other, unto the tens of millions, we would not only die—which has a purpose—but we would depart existence, which would be meaningless.

"The nature of the prairie is abundance beyond belief. That richness is portioned out to support life. Within the system none is more important than the other.

"If an invader, such as a tree, comes into the prairie, it consumes more than its share and temporarily cuts off nourishment for others. It takes root and grows a few years, proudly taller and stronger than plants around it.

"The fire will come, and the tree will die. Other, less sturdy vegetation, with roots deeper in the soil, will survive.

"Ojuiba was of the prairie. The Indians are of the prairie. All humankind can be of the prairie.

"Be as the plant or the Indian and you will survive. The person you knew as Ojuiba blossomed here and is yet a flower in existence, whose seeds are upon your moccasins to be carried throughout the world."

***

A hand grabbed my shoulder roughly. I turned around. It was Major Richard Thoreau of the United States Army.

Official

United States Army of Occupation: June 30, 1984

CHICAGOU, INDIAN NATION: A spokesman for this office to-day issued an official denial of the authenticity of a manuscript being circulated and attributed to the late Silas P. Bigelow, reporter for the *Philadelphia Gazette*. Major Richard Thoreau, liaison officer for information, called the document "a total fabrication, pure sedition."

"I knew Si Bigelow personally," Major Thoreau said. "These writings represent the opposite of his thinking. These 'autobiographical' notes are clearly a ploy to identify him with the destructive 'passive resistance' movement among the Indians rather than with the country he loved.

"When we found him, he was in bad physical and mental condition. He was living in a field, undernourished and hallucinating. He thought we had come to kill passenger pigeons rather than to save him.

"In his memory we ask that all copies of the manuscript be turned over to the government or be destroyed."